VICTORIAN
MANSION
FLOWER SHOP
MYSTERIES™

Absent Without Leaf

Sandra Orchard

AnniesFiction.com

Books in the Victorian Mansion Flower Shop Mysteries series

Library of Congress-in-Publication Data
Absent Without Leaf / by Sandra Orchard
p. cm.
I. Title
                    2019937952

AnniesFiction.com
(800) 282-6643
Victorian Mansion Flower Shop Mysteries™
Series Creators: Shari Lohner, Janice Tate
Editor: Elizabeth Morrissey
Cover Illustrator: Bob Kayganich

10 11 12 13 14 | Printed in China | 9 8 7 6 5 4 3

1

"This is crazy." Kaylee Bleu frowned and swept a long, dark strand of hair out of her eyes. "How can no one know who owns one of the largest estates on Orcas Island?" she demanded of her fellow members of the Petal Pushers garden club.

Mary Bishop cleared her throat. "I remember when Pennybrook Grove was owned by the Merchant family. They'd call every so often with a trespasser complaint." Mary had been a 911 dispatcher for the island's sheriff's department before retiring and becoming a part-time employee at Kaylee's florist shop, The Flower Patch. "But I have no idea who bought it after Herbert Merchant passed away five or six years ago."

The furrow in Kaylee's brow deepened. "Spring break is next week for Turtle Cove schools, and I've already reserved a bus to drive us all to see the tree." She picked up her clipboard, incredulously scanning the agenda secured to its surface. "How will it look if we have to cancel our horticultural camp's first outing?"

Bakery owner Jessica Roberts moved to the window of the Old Cape Lighthouse keeper's quarters and gazed across West Sound toward the twenty-acre gated property in question. "If you ask me, the town should've bought the place and designated it as a conservation area. They could've used the mansion as a museum or something. I mean, what's the point of knowing where the island's oldest tree stands if no one can see it?"

"The clerk at the town office said it was bought by a trust five years ago," DeeDee Wilcox explained. The mystery bookshop owner and mother of two school-age daughters had been given the task of securing permission for the excursion. "The best she could do was give me their lawyer's contact information. But when I tried calling him, his receptionist said he's on vacation and no one else there has the authority to tell me what I want to know."

Kaylee's little dachshund, Bear, must have sensed the discouragement in DeeDee's voice, because he sat beside her chair and pawed at her knee, as if to say she'd done her best. With a smile, DeeDee bent to give him an affectionate pat. "Thanks, buddy."

"Which law firm?" Mary asked.

"I don't remember the name, but it's in Washington, D.C." DeeDee put a knowing emphasis on the location.

Mary sighed. "Then we're probably looking at a politician."

"And somehow I doubt anyone who's that protective of his or her privacy is going to give us permission anyway." Jessica paced the floor, studying her own clipboard. Her short, black hair bounced with her movements, the glossy locks glistening under the overhead lights. "Maybe we should move up the field trip to The Flower Patch from later in the week to Monday. That would at least give us more time to come up with another activity."

"But we anchored the whole theme of the camp on the tree's story," Kaylee said, frustration edging her voice.

While the women discussed their dilemma, Jessica's twenty-something daughter, Mila, slipped into the room. She shared Jessica's dark eyes and hair, courtesy of their Japanese-American heritage, as well as her mother's spunky personality. As she tiptoed toward her mom, she dropped a set of keys, which clanged noisily against the hardwood floor. "Whoops," Mila said as she bent to retrieve the keys. "So much for being sneaky."

Mary laughed. "You can't sneak in and out of here without telling us what you're up to, young lady."

"Mila needs to borrow my SUV to pick up a bureau she bought from a resale shop in Eastsound for her new apartment," Jessica said, digging in her purse for her own keys. "I get to zip home in her Mini Cooper tonight."

"A new place?" DeeDee asked. "Are you moving back to Orcas Island?"

"No, it's just a bigger place in Seattle," Mila said as she and Jessica swapped key rings.

"And in a safer neighborhood," Jessica added.

Mila smiled at her mother. "Closer to my new job too."

"Congratulations," Kaylee said. "What's the new job?"

"I'll be working for one of the big tech companies," Mila explained. "My official title is Community Outreach Administrator, but it's just a fancy way of saying I'll get to coordinate the company's participation in community events and advise the bosses on which local charities to donate their money to."

"That's great!" Kaylee, Mary, and DeeDee crowed in unison.

"And maybe eventually she can move back here and tele-commute," Jessica said, earning an indulgent eye roll from her daughter. "In the meantime, Luke and I get to enjoy having her visit for a couple of weeks."

"You're all invited to come see the new place once I've moved in," Mila said graciously, then hitched her thumb toward the door. "I'd better get going. Sorry for interrupting the meeting."

Among a chorus of goodbyes, Mila headed for the door.

DeeDee circled their discussion back to the tree. "When I drove to the estate the week before last, the house — at least what I could see of it through the trees — looked completely deserted. The neighbor wasn't around either, so chances are no one would be the wiser if we just drove the kids out there."

"Having our group cited for trespassing would *not* be a good start to our spring break camp," Mary said. "Seeing the island's oldest tree isn't worth ending up in jail."

Mila stopped in the doorway. "Are you talking about the tree out at Pennybrook Grove?"

"Yes," Kaylee said. "Do you know who owns the property?"

"No, but I used to date their neighbor, Tad Mason. He'd probably know."

Jessica's eyes widened. "I didn't realize the Masons lived next door to the estate. I thought he and his mom lived in town. I guess it's been a while since I talked to Tabitha."

"They moved out there after Tad's dad died," Mila said. "But Tad doesn't live there currently. He's in grad school out east."

"Would you mind asking Tad if he knows his neighbors?" Jessica asked.

Regret colored Mila's pretty face. "I don't know his number anymore, and he's not on social media." Her expression brightened a little. "I could call his mom if you like and see what she knows."

"Wait, are we talking about Tabitha Mason?" Mary asked. When Mila nodded, Mary beamed. "Then I think we're in luck. Tad phoned in an order for a flower arrangement to be delivered on her birthday tomorrow. He gave me the address, but I didn't realize their house neighbored Pennybrook Grove."

"That's perfect." Kaylee flipped up her itinerary and jotted a reminder on the notepad behind it. "Thanks for the offer to call her, Mila, but I'm making tomorrow morning's flower deliveries. I can ask Tabitha Mason myself if she can help us contact her reclusive neighbors."

Mila opened the door. "No problem. See you later."

As Mila was exiting, she held the door as schoolteacher Sara Wright bustled in.

"Sorry I'm late," Sara said. "I'm coaching the middle school girls volleyball team and our game went long." She shrugged out of her coat and finger-combed her windblown red hair back into a perfect bob.

Mary shooed away her apology with a wave of her hand. "We're just grateful for your experienced help with the spring break camp. Most teachers would be desperate for a week off."

Sara shook her head. "I love the kids. And since the camp is only in the afternoons, I still get to sleep in. As long as I don't have to grade papers, it's all good."

The group chuckled, then launched into a discussion about the other activities planned for their camp. After confirming the schedule of events and the role each woman would play, Kaylee reached into her tote for a manila folder.

"I've compiled lists of the supplies we still need," Kaylee said. She handed the food list to Jessica, who had volunteered her staff at Death by Chocolate to provide the camp's snacks.

"I'll take the book list," DeeDee offered. She scanned the paper Kaylee gave her. "Looks like my next stop is the public library."

"Arts and crafts or plant gathering?" Kaylee asked Sara, holding out both lists to the teacher.

Sara scanned both lists quickly. "I'll take the arts and crafts."

"Are you sure?" Mary asked.

"Absolutely. You and Kaylee can take care of the plant gathering. I doubt you have the ones on that list on hand in the flower shop."

"You're right," Kaylee agreed. "We'll have to comb the meadows for the wild plants. At least we can enlist the kids' help in finding some of them." She straightened her stack of notes. "Okay, looks as if we're done for the night." She summoned Bear and snapped on his lead. "See all of you here on Saturday for registration?"

Everyone agreed, then grabbed their coats and headed out. Kaylee and Mary hopped into Kaylee's red Ford Escape for the return trip to The Flower Patch, where Mary had left her car. Kaylee started the engine and flipped on her headlights. Thanks to the recent time change, twilight still lingered, but the streets were quiet.

As they drove past The Sunfish Café, a man clutching a

yellow rain slicker stepped out of the restaurant and into the road.

Kaylee slammed on her brakes with a shriek. The Escape stopped a couple feet away from the man, and Kaylee thanked her lucky stars that she'd recently replaced the brakes as her heart pounded.

The man gave her a little wave of thanks as he crossed in front of her car, then he stopped on the other side and glanced up and down the street. At the blast of the ferry whistle, he seemed to come to a decision and strode toward the water.

"I heard we're supposed to get as much as an inch of rain tonight," Mary said, apparently having paid more attention to the man's unworn rain slicker than the fact that he'd walked out in front of them.

"It can rain all it wants now," Kaylee said as she eased the car forward again. "As long as it's dry for our camp."

The next morning, Kaylee decided to drive past Tabitha Mason's house to check out Pennybrook Grove before delivering Tabitha's flowers. "Maybe we'll get lucky and find them home," Kaylee said to Bear, who was watching the scenery sweep past the side window.

Kaylee hadn't been to the property herself since she was a young girl, about the age their campers would be. Growing up, visiting her grandparents on the island had always been a summer highlight for her and her brother, Kyle. And since their grandmother, Bea Lyons, had run The Flower Patch for so many years before selling it to Kaylee so she could retire, she'd seemed to know everyone, including Herbert Merchant, who had owned the estate at that time.

Although she had fleeting memories of the family, what had stuck most in Kaylee's recollection was her absolute awe of the old tree, and her surprise that the tallest tree on the property, a towering Douglas fir, wasn't the oldest. She hoped they still had the giant *Pseudotsuga menziesii* too, as its size would make for another good lesson. For that matter, so would teaching the children some of the trees' Latin names. After years of teaching plant taxonomy at the University of Washington, it was second nature to Kaylee to think of plants by their scientific names.

Spotting the driveway, she flicked on her signal, only to be blocked by a locked gate at the entrance. She stopped without turning in and peered down the long winding driveway, but she couldn't see the mansion. The majestic Douglas fir she remembered so well still stood head and shoulders above the rest of the trees. Anticipation flowed through her as she thought of how rewarding the field trip could be, if only they could gain access to the property.

They'd have to keep a close eye on the students, of course, since the property sat on a bluff overlooking the rocky shore—the one side that wasn't fenced—but Sara was used to reining in children.

Kaylee turned the delivery van around, then returned the way she'd come and parked in Tabitha Mason's driveway. Grabbing the colorful spring bouquet she'd made, Kaylee wagged a finger at her prancing dog. "Sorry to burst your bubble, but you're staying here. I'll only be a minute."

But one minute turned into three, then five. After her third knock went unanswered, Kaylee wandered around the side of the house to peek in the garage. It was empty.

She tried the garage's side door, hoping she could leave the flowers for Tabitha on a bench inside, but it was locked. Kaylee eyed the large rolling door, but decided against trying to open it. Somehow going that far felt too much like an invasion of privacy.

As she contemplated her next step, a calico cat with wet fur and a pink collar twined around her legs, mewing loudly. Kaylee bent down and gave her some attention. "Hello there. Do you live here?"

Barking erupted from Kaylee's delivery van. Kaylee instinctively said "shush," not that Bear likely heard it over all the noise he was making. He stood on the passenger seat, craning for a better view of Kaylee's new friend. "Don't worry, Bear. I'm not bringing her home."

The cat mewed mournfully.

"He actually likes cats," Kaylee cooed, giving the feline another affectionate rub, "but I'm sure your mistress will be home soon." Straightening, she glanced around. "Let's see if there's a back porch where I can leave these flowers in the meantime."

The day's mild weather wouldn't hurt the spring arrangement, but she wasn't so sure she could say the same for the cat. Kaylee let herself in through the back gate and walked toward the house, but there was nothing more than a small slab of cement by the back door.

"So much for the porch idea," she said to the cat. Kaylee pulled a card that said *Sorry we missed you* from her pocket and jotted in the date and time she'd attempted delivery.

Judging by the fact that the rear entrance was more easily accessible from the driveway than the front door, she tucked the card in the jamb of the back door instead of walking to the front porch to leave it there. "Now don't you climb up and take it," she joked to the cat.

While the cat milled around, casting occasional glances at the delivery van where Bear kept up his vigilant watch, Kaylee took in Tabitha's backyard. The grass had already turned green, and birdsong filled the air. An impressive variety of perennials were already growing vigorously in the wide flower beds bordering the property fence. On the other side of the fence, shrubs and trees ensured the Pennybrook Grove owner's privacy, but also made Tabitha's secluded space feel like a peaceful sanctuary. Kaylee could even hear the soothing splash of waves in the distance.

A flash of bright green beyond the trees on the other side of the fence snagged Kaylee's attention. Most of the summer people hired groundskeepers to take care of their properties during the rest of the year. If that was who she'd seen, maybe he could give her the owner's contact information. Kaylee peered up and down the fence line, looking for a break in the trees through which she might spot the person again. But the flower beds bordering Tabitha's side of the fence made it awkward. The last thing Kaylee wanted to do was inadvertently step on Tabitha's soon-to-bloom tulips. Toward the back of the yard, she finally found a break in the foliage. And from the looks of the adjoining swath of crushed plants, so had Tabitha's cat.

"Did you do this?" Kaylee asked the calico, who had trailed her.

Unsurprisingly, the cat ignored her.

Kaylee gingerly stepped around the trampled flowers and up to the fence. Standing on her tiptoes, she peered every which way until she caught sight of a woman in a bright-green jacket, wearing gardening gloves and carrying a hand spade.

"Excuse me!" Kaylee called out.

Instead of responding, the woman wandered off to a circular flower bed deeper in the yard, apparently deaf to Kaylee's call.

Kaylee tried calling once more over the fence, but she'd already lost sight of the woman. Glancing toward Pennybrook Grove's gate, which was several yards away, Kaylee weighed her options: hop the fence and catch up to the woman before she disappeared entirely, or go around and rattle the driveway's gate until someone let her in.

The woman stepped back into view.

Kaylee waved her arm. "Excuse me!" She set Tabitha's floral arrangement on the ground next to the fence and then clambered over.

The woman still hadn't noticed Kaylee—or if she had, she was doing an impressive job of ignoring her.

"Excuse me." Kaylee waved again and hurried toward the woman. "I was hoping to talk to you."

The woman pivoted abruptly, her eyes wide. She tugged on a wire near her chin and pulled out a pair of earbuds. The tinny sound of music humming from them reassured Kaylee that the woman had honestly not heard her before that moment.

"I'm Kaylee Bleu." She offered a hand. "I'm the owner of The Flower Patch."

"How did you get on this property?" the woman demanded, ignoring Kaylee's gesture. "We don't need any flowers. Thank you."

Kaylee's offered handshake turned into an apologetic wave. "Oh no, I'm not here to try to sell you anything. I was hoping you could help me contact the estate's owner. You see, our garden club is—"

The woman's gaze shifted to something beyond Kaylee's right shoulder. Kaylee's skin prickled and the rest of her explanation stuck in her throat.

Footfalls thudded on the ground, faster and louder by the second.

Kaylee spun around.

A man, gun drawn, raced toward her.

Her hands shot into the air. "No, wait! I'm just a florist!"

2

The linebacker-size man tackled her, and Kaylee hit the dirt.

"What are you doing? Get off me!" she yelled. "I wasn't hurting anyone. I just had a question."

"Pull her up," a gruff male voice ordered from somewhere nearby.

The voice sounded vaguely familiar and the instant her attacker hauled her off the ground, Kaylee realized why. "Phil? Phil Haynes? It's me, Kaylee Bleu. Your sister's college roommate."

The frown marring Phil's handsome features transformed swiftly into a smile. "Kaylee? Hey, good to see you." To the man who still held Kaylee's arm, he said, "You can release her. She's not our prowler." His attention returned to Kaylee. "Or have you taken up a life of crime I don't know about? The last I heard, you were a professor and forensic botany consultant for the Seattle police department."

Kaylee's heart gave a silly little kick that the man had actually discussed her with his sister, Brynn, who was ten years younger. Back in their college days, Kaylee had had a major crush on the tall, dark-haired, brown-eyed guy who would periodically give them a welcome respite from residence food by taking them out for dinner.

"What are you doing here?" Phil prodded, jolting Kaylee out of her walk down memory lane.

"Oh," Kaylee said, willing herself not to stutter. "Well, my position at the university got eliminated a couple of years ago, and my grandmother invited me to come to Orcas Island to take over her flower shop. I'd always loved my visits here growing up, so how could I refuse?"

"I was asking what you're doing *here*," he said, gesturing at the ground. "But yeah—Brynn didn't tell me you live on Orcas Island, or I would've looked you up."

"I'm sure she has her hands full with those twins," Kaylee said, ignoring a twinge of longing. It had been a long time since she'd visited her old friend. Pushing the thought aside, her brow furrowed. "What are *you* doing here?"

Phil flicked his hand at the other man—his colleague, maybe? "You can return to your post. I've got this."

The burly man slanted a sideways glance at Kaylee, appearing less than confident. Then, without a word, he headed through the trees, toward the house if Kaylee remembered correctly. The woman followed, also silent.

"Do you still work for the National Security Agency?" Kaylee asked. "Let me guess—I breached the perimeter on some secret meeting involving the president."

Phil laughed out loud. "It's not quite that bad. You just startled the admiral's wife while she was tending her garden."

Kaylee gaped after the woman in the bright-green jacket. "You mean she lives here? I thought she was the groundskeeper. The Petal Pushers have been trying to contact the residents here for weeks. But no one seemed to know who owned the place."

Phil quirked an eyebrow. "The Petal Pushers?"

"The garden club I belong to. We're hosting a spring break camp for elementary school kids next week, and we wanted to bring them here on a field trip to see the island's oldest tree." Kaylee winced at the memory of the less-than-stellar impression she'd made on the owner. "You said admiral?"

"Yes, Rear Admiral Robert Newton."

"I take it he's pretty important?"

Phil's smile didn't reach his eyes. "He's about to become the admiral of the naval fleet in Hawaii."

Kaylee's heart sank. The likelihood of being able to bring her campers here seemed to be taking a nosedive. "So you're here to ensure any would-be prowlers don't make off with documents critical to our national security?"

"How many campers will you have?" Phil asked, apparently deciding her question didn't warrant an answer. Or maybe it was one of those "I could tell you, but then I'd have to kill you" scenarios.

Kaylee studied his all-business expression and opted not to tease him—especially not if he was about to offer to help her. "Registration is tomorrow, but we anticipate about thirty kids between seven and ten years old. And we'll have at least one adult supervising every ten campers."

Although Phil's sober expression didn't offer the encouragement she'd have liked to see, he surprised her by saying, "Come with me. I'll introduce you to Rear Admiral Newton and you can ask him yourself."

Phil cupped her elbow in his hand and led her through the impressive arboretum—an exquisite collection of everything from *Arbutus menziesii* to *Pyrus communis*. Eventually, the Pacific madrone and wild pear trees gave way to a clearing overlooking the bluffs above West Sound. A massive two-story stone house surrounded by cascading rock gardens dominated the open space.

A long-legged, thirtysomething man, whose sandy blond highlights looked as if they came from a bottle rather than the sun, sauntered across the yard toward them. "Are you going to introduce me to your friend?" he asked Phil, his gaze never releasing its lock on Kaylee.

"This is Kaylee Bleu, an old friend of mine," Phil told the young man. "Kaylee, meet Ryan Newton, the admiral's son. He's been crashing here for the past couple of weeks." He cleared his throat. "While he's between jobs."

Kaylee nodded. "I see."

Ryan shook her hand. "Do you have dinner plans?"

Kaylee was caught off guard by the abrupt invitation and couldn't think of a response. She must've looked like a deer caught in the headlights, because Phil spoke up on her behalf.

"Now's not a good time, Ryan," he said.

Ryan glanced back at the house, where a distinguished man stood on the porch with rigid posture. Ryan saluted Phil. "Got it," he said, then turned on his heel and headed in the opposite direction.

"I wouldn't recommend spending your time on that one," Phil murmured to Kaylee.

"Likes to play the field?"

"That's putting it kindly."

Rear Admiral Newton strode over to them. Up close, he was an imposing figure at six feet and then some. From his salt-and-pepper hair and finely-lined face, Kaylee pegged him at being in his mid to late fifties. "What's going on, Haynes?" the man demanded. "Diane said this woman came over the fence."

"I'm sorry, sir," Kaylee said. "I called out to your wife to try to get her attention, but she didn't hear me. I'm afraid I climbed over without thinking."

"This is Kaylee Bleu, sir," Phil said. "She's heading up a horticulture camp for schoolchildren next week and would like permission to bring them here to see the island's oldest tree."

"Out of the question," the admiral said firmly without a second's hesitation.

"Sir, I understand your concern," Phil said, "but I wouldn't consider a group of children to pose a threat."

"Of course not, but—"

"Mark and I will be here to keep our eyes on them," Phil continued.

The admiral sputtered a few more protests, but Phil deflected them like a champion jouster and finally earned consent.

"Keep the children out of Diane's flower beds," the admiral barked, then strode back to the house.

"Wow," Kaylee said when the admiral was out of earshot. "Your talent might be wasted on security detail, Phil. You should be a negotiator."

He grinned, and this time light sparkled in his eyes. "It was the least I could do after the unceremonious welcome we gave you. I'll walk you out." He guided her toward the driveway.

Kaylee stopped short as a small parking area came into view, recognizing a black Ford pickup with a massive toolbox in the bed. "Reese is working for the admiral?"

Phil raised an eyebrow. "Reese?"

Kaylee motioned to the truck. "Reese Holt, Turtle Cove's favorite handyman." *And handsomest,* a little voice added in her mind.

"Right, yes. He's repairing a broken window."

Kaylee squinted at the windows she could see from this side of the house, but the broken one must've been on another side.

Phil tugged on her elbow. "Coming?"

She pictured Pennybrook Grove's long, winding driveway and then the subsequent walk down the road to Tabitha Mason's. "Actually, I'm parked next door. I was delivering a flower arrangement. It'd be quicker to cut across the yard and go back over the fence the way I came—oh no!" Remembering Bear in the van, Kaylee sucked in a breath. "My dog will be wondering where I am."

"Did you talk to the person who lives next door?" Phil asked, his brusque tone stunning Kaylee into silence. Without waiting for a response, Phil steered her into the copse of trees behind the house. "There was a prowler on the grounds yesterday evening. We'd hoped to ask the neighbor if she saw anything, but she wasn't home when we stopped by."

"A prowler? Is that how the window got broken?" Kaylee peered through the trees and caught a glimpse of Reese working on a narrow window beside the back door.

"Yes." Phil's hold shifted from her elbow to the small of her back with a gentle push, urging her to pick up the pace.

The possible significance of the trampled flowers she'd seen suddenly dawned on Kaylee and she gasped.

"What is it?" Phil asked.

Kaylee explained about the flowers. "But Tabitha Mason isn't home right now either." Kaylee's eyes widened as a worse thought struck her. "In fact, her cat came up to me bedraggled and wet from being left out in the rain. What if Tabitha saw something she shouldn't have yesterday and the prowler hurt her?"

A strangled squeak drew Kaylee's attention to her left where Diane Newton was kneeling over a nearby flower bed, apparently listening in on their conversation. The woman ducked her head and attacked the dirt with a vengeance. *The poor woman. Last night's trespasser must have her wound up tighter than a ten-day clock.*

Leading Kaylee back through the trees, Phil said, "There was no vehicle in the driveway or garage when I checked the place."

"There still isn't. Maybe she's at work or away. But you'd think she'd have left some shelter for the cat."

When they reached the break in the trees that marked where Kaylee had vaulted the fence, they both climbed over, and Kaylee pointed out the trampled plants to Phil. Upon close inspection, they had clearly been trodden on by a person, not the cat.

"This could be how your prowler got in and out," Kaylee said. "Look, these footprints are mine." She held her foot over one to show how her shoe matched the size and shape. "But these other prints head both toward the fence and away from it." They were bigger than Kaylee's, but an average size for a man.

Phil squatted and snapped pictures of the markings with his cell phone.

"Did the prowler get away with confidential files or something?" Kaylee asked.

Phil pushed to his feet. "I'm not at liberty to discuss the incident."

"Of course. I understand." Kaylee retrieved the flower arrangement she'd left sitting beside the fence. "I guess I'll take these back to the shop and wait to hear from Mrs. Mason."

"Who ordered the flowers for Mrs. Mason?" Phil sounded less like an old friend and more like an investigator.

"Her son," Kaylee answered. "For her birthday."

"Do you have his phone number?"

"It should be on the delivery sheet in the van. Why?"

Phil scraped his hand across his bristly chin with a reluctant sigh. "Her son clearly expected her to be home this morning."

Kaylee grimaced. "Good point. Follow me. I can give him a call right now."

As Kaylee crossed the backyard toward the gate, she scanned the grounds and trees for the cat that had refused to leave her alone when she'd first arrived. She spotted it cowering under a shrub, eyeing Phil warily, and an icy chill shivered down Kaylee's spine at the thought of what the cat might've seen the last man in her backyard do.

Bear lay contentedly dozing on the passenger seat of the delivery van. When she opened the door, he slowly stretched himself awake—until he spotted Phil, at which point he hopped to the ground and issued a few sharp barks.

"Hush, Bear, it's okay," Kaylee reassured her pint-size protector. "Phil is an old friend." She grabbed the end of his leash and passed it to Phil. "Could you please walk him around a bit while I make the call?"

Bear's nose was already on the ground, probably onto the cat's scent. He tugged Phil toward the backyard.

"Don't let him near the cat," she called after them as she dialed. "He'll want to get close to her, and I think she's been through enough."

Tad Mason answered his phone on the third ring. "She should be home," he said in response to Kaylee's query. "She cleans houses, but she said her Friday client gave her the day off so she could enjoy a long weekend."

"Is it possible that she went away somewhere for an impromptu birthday celebration with a friend?" Kaylee asked.

"I'd say yes, but she never leaves Peony out overnight. And she always has a friend check on the cat if she's gone."

"Her car isn't here," Kaylee said.

"This doesn't make sense." Tad was starting to sound alarmed. "She wouldn't have left the cat out if she didn't plan to come home. Can you hold on? I'll try her cell phone." He disconnected their call, but called Kaylee back within a minute or so. "It went straight to voice mail."

Kaylee sighed. "I didn't want to worry you, but the estate next door had a prowler incident last night. So the fact that you expected her to be here is a little disconcerting."

"Her car might be at the mechanic's. She said it needed some work. Would you mind checking inside the house for me?"

"It's locked."

"That's weird. She doesn't usually bother locking it."

Kaylee walked up the driveway and through the back gate. "Perhaps she keeps a spare key hidden outside?" She spotted a flowerpot next to the back door. "Oh, I think I found it."

The pot had a dry spot beside it as if it had been moved,

while the rest of the cement stoop it stood on was still wet from last night's rain. She tipped the pot to glance under it, but there was nothing underneath. "Did you find the spare key?" she called to Phil, who was being led by Bear around the backyard.

"Me? No." He gave Bear's leash a gentle tug and headed Kaylee's way. "Did her son say there was one?"

"Yes." Kaylee held up her finger to silence Phil and lifted the phone she'd been muting against her jacket. "Sorry, Tad. It wasn't under the flowerpot."

"She doesn't keep it there," Tad explained. "Do you see a frog statue in the flower bed next to the back door?"

"Yes." Kaylee pointed it out to Phil, who went over to investigate.

Phil stooped down and stretched his fingers inside the frog's mouth. "Ouch!" he yelped, yanking his hand back. Then he grinned. "Just kidding." He held up the key victoriously. "We're in."

"Found it," Kaylee said to Tad. "I'll go in and check around, then call you back." Disconnecting the call, she prayed she wasn't about to discover anything Tad wouldn't want to know.

3

Kaylee tried knocking on the back door one last time. Still receiving no answer, she inserted the key. Cracking open the door, she called Tabitha's name. No response.

Peony dashed past Kaylee's legs and into the warm house.

Kaylee glanced at Phil. "If the gate's closed, Bear will be fine in the backyard while we check the place out." She wasn't sure if Phil had intended to join her in walking through the house, but she preferred not to do it alone.

Phil frowned. "I'd rather not leave the dog loose back here. He might destroy evidence."

"Good point." Kaylee took Bear's leash from him and looped the handle around the gatepost. "Stay."

Bear immediately sat, and Phil appeared impressed.

Kaylee gave the dog an affectionate rub behind the ears and promised him a treat when she was done, then returned to the back door. Pushing the door all the way open, Kaylee called Tabitha's name once more as she entered into a bright, airy, eat-in kitchen, with white cupboards and a gleaming white floor—minus the dirty paw prints leading to a food dish next to the refrigerator, where Peony was happily munching on kibble Tabitha must have left out for her.

A pair of sneakers and a pair of rain boots sat in a neat line on a boot mat behind the door. Kaylee toed off her shoes so as not to track dirt through the house, and Phil followed suit. The coatrack on the wall above the boot tray held a purple winter coat on one hook and a lightweight purple windbreaker-type jacket on the hook beside it. A third hook was empty.

Kaylee padded down the short hall that bypassed the kitchen to a combination living room and office. One wall had built-in, floor-to-ceiling bookcases flanking a stone fireplace. A Colonial-style desk filled much of the space in front of the window. A high school graduation photo of a young man Kaylee presumed to be Tad was positioned on the far corner of the desk, and an ornate banker's lamp rested opposite. A hand-painted coaster signed *Tad* that looked as if it might've dated to his primary school days sat to the left of the desk blotter, making Kaylee wonder if Tabitha was left-handed or merely held her mug with her left hand so she could keep using her right.

"What is it?" Phil asked.

Kaylee shook away the thought. "Nothing. Just admiring the coaster her son must've painted for her when he was little."

A burgundy leather sofa and two coordinating armchairs dominated the rest of the room, and a small TV stood on an end table tucked into the corner. There wasn't a speck of dust to be seen—not surprising for a professional house cleaner—although the armchair closest to the fireplace was clearly the cat's domain, as it had a fur-encrusted cloth laid over the seat.

Still nervous as to what she might find, Kaylee took a deep breath before following Phil past the small front foyer and down the hall toward the bedrooms. The first door on the right belonged to the bathroom. A purple bath towel and hand towel hung neatly folded on the bar and a matching shag rug lay in front of the tub. The next door opened into the master bedroom, and at the sight of the neatly made bed, Kaylee released the breath she'd been holding. The drapes were open.

Phil checked the closet. "Nothing out of the ordinary here."

Kaylee glanced inside. Even the clothes were meticulously arranged according to color. "Tabitha certainly keeps a tidy house."

She smiled appreciatively, then analyzed the rest of the room.

The uncluttered top and smudge-free surface of the mirrored dresser made the place look as unlived-in as the woman's desk. Kaylee seemed to have a catchall dish or jar in every room—one for pencils and paper clips on her desk, one for coins and hair ties on her dresser, and one for keys and coupons in her kitchen. Tabitha had only a jewelry box, the cleanest brush and comb set Kaylee had ever seen outside a store, and a framed wedding photo.

Phil paused at the foot of the bed and gestured toward the abundance of solid purple and floral throw pillows. "Three guesses what this lady's favorite color is."

"You call yourself an agent?" Kaylee teased. "I figured that out with one look at her coatrack the minute we came in."

The lone door on the opposite side of the hall opened into a boy's bedroom. Trophies and framed award certificates filled the shelves and wall.

"Looks as if her son's a smart kid." Phil slipped past Kaylee and headed for the closet.

Two shirts and a pair of black dress pants hung in the closet, and an old pair of soccer cleats sat on the floor.

Kaylee shook her head. "I moved out of my parents' house over twenty years ago and, until they moved to Florida, they still had more of my stuff in my old room than this."

"Hmm," Phil said. "That could explain the unlived-in vibe I'm getting. Maybe she's had her house staged in preparation for putting it on the market."

"Or she's just bringing her work home with her," Kaylee said. "Some people can't relax in a dirty house."

The last room to check was behind a door off the kitchen. The small space housed the furnace, the hot water tank, and the laundry facilities. Phil pointed to the shelf above the washing machine, which was filled with a row of suitcases in descending sizes. "All her luggage appears to be here."

Kaylee pulled out her phone. "I'd better call Tad back. He'll be worried about what's taking me so long. At least there's no sign of any kind of struggle. Tabitha probably just went away without telling her son." Kaylee glanced at the row of luggage that begged to differ. Except the luggage was all black. "I bet you if she weren't away, we'd find a purple overnight bag in her closet."

"Ask her son," Phil said, squeezing out of the furnace room. As Kaylee called Tad, Phil opened the refrigerator door. "Nix that. A woman going on a getaway doesn't leave a steak marinating in her fridge."

While the line rang, Kaylee peeked over his shoulder and sniffed. "It must be fresh. It doesn't smell as if it's going bad."

Phil pulled a hunk of plastic wrap from the top of the trash can and examined the label. "The steak was packaged yesterday."

After Tad picked up, Kaylee relayed what she and Phil had and hadn't discovered.

"Where could she be?" Tad asked, sounding lost.

"Perhaps you should call the sheriff's office to report her missing," Kaylee suggested gently, feeling bad for the obviously concerned young man. "They could put out a BOLO for her license plate."

"Yes. Yes, I'll do that," Tad said, his voice still anxious.

"And I can swing past here again after work to see if she's returned and to check on the cat," Kaylee offered.

"Thank you, Ms. Bleu," Tad said distractedly, then disconnected the call.

"What can you tell me about this woman?" Phil asked Kaylee. He removed the calendar from the wall next to Tabitha's refrigerator and leafed through the previous months, no doubt making mental notes about every appointment.

"Nothing." Kaylee glanced around the room. "I'm not even sure what she looks like, except maybe an older version of the blonde in the wedding photo in her room—if that's even her." Kaylee pulled a business card and pen from her pocket and jotted Tad's cell phone number on the back. "This is her son's number. He'll be better able to answer your questions."

Phil flipped over the card and read the information on the front. "This is your flower shop?"

"Yes." She took the card back and jotted her mobile number on the bottom before giving it to Phil again. "That's my cell number if you need to reach me." She smiled. "Or if you want to go to lunch and catch up one of these days."

"Thanks," Phil said, pocketing the card.

"I know you're busy, but it'd be great to see you again before you leave the island," she said as she locked the house and returned the key to its hiding place.

"You can count on it." He gave her a warm hug, and Bear whined slightly. Chuckling, Phil stepped back, his hands raised in surrender, and gave Kaylee a wink. "She's all yours, Bear. For the moment, anyway."

"Good news," Kaylee said to Mary the instant she and Bear walked into The Flower Patch's front area. "The field trip to view the island's oldest tree is a go."

DeeDee, who stood at the counter with Mary, gaped at Kaylee. "How did you manage to pull off in one morning what I couldn't do in over a month?"

Kaylee shrugged. "Chalk it up to serendipity."

"Well, let's hope whatever Jess has to say won't spoil our new winning streak," DeeDee said. "She wants to see us all next door ASAP."

Kaylee and Mary exchanged a glance. "We shouldn't both leave," Kaylee said. "Who will watch the shop?"

DeeDee motioned to the quiet sales floor. "This place is empty. The street is empty. Just put a sign on the door saying you'll be back later."

"She's right. We haven't had a single customer all morning." Mary dug their movable clock sign out from under the counter and handed it to Kaylee.

"Okay, let's go find out what Jess wants to see us about." Kaylee steered Bear toward his bed. "You can have a nap. We won't be long." She adjusted the return time on the clock to a half hour later and hung it on the front door, then the three friends exited and walked next door to Death by Chocolate.

"They're here," Jessica's assistant, Gretchen, called into the kitchen when Kaylee, DeeDee, and Mary entered the bakery and coffee shop.

Jessica bustled out of the kitchen wiping her flour-covered hands on her apron. "Thanks for coming so quickly." She motioned to an empty table by the counter. "Let's sit here."

"What's going on?" Mary asked.

"Do you remember Tad Mason?" Jessica asked and Kaylee's heart skipped a beat.

"Sure," Mary said. "Isn't he the young man who took Mila to the high school prom? He ordered the most gorgeous wrist corsage for her. Bea and I had the best time making it." Mary cocked her head. "Didn't Mila say that his mother lives next door to Pennybrook Grove?"

"That's right," Jessica said. "Tad is in Washington, D.C., at the moment, completing an internship as part of his postgraduate studies, and he just called me, beside himself with worry. It's his mother's birthday and he can't reach her. He called me and said he had someone check the house and there's no sign of Tabitha or the car."

Kaylee raised her hand. "I was the someone who checked the house."

"Of course." Jessica smacked herself in the forehead. "I knew you were taking flowers out there this morning. I didn't put two and two together."

"You never told me she wasn't home," Mary said to Kaylee. Kaylee gave a wry smile. "I never had the chance."

"So," Jessica continued, "Tad said that because there was no sign of foul play and Tabitha doesn't have any kind of medical condition to be concerned about, the sheriff's deputy Tad spoke to all but dismissed his concerns, saying his mother could've simply gone away for a few days without telling him and forgotten to charge her phone." Jessica turned pleading eyes on Kaylee. "You must've heard how frantic he is. He said he can't get away for at least a few more days and he begged me to do whatever I can. I was hoping you could all help."

"Of course," DeeDee said. "What do you want us to do?"

Jessica beamed at her gratefully. "We could start by making posters to pin up in our shops."

"Do you have a picture of Tabitha?" Kaylee asked. "I didn't see any on display in her house."

Jessica's smile faded. "No."

"I'm sure I can find one online." DeeDee pulled out her smartphone and began tapping at the screen.

While DeeDee peered at her phone, Jessica went on. "Tad said he called their usual cat sitter and his mother hadn't asked her to look in on Peony, which makes him all the more convinced Tabitha didn't go away."

"I'm sure he's right," Kaylee agreed. "She had a steak marinating in the fridge."

Jessica bit her bottom lip, clearly disturbed by the additional information. "I was thinking we could ask around, try to figure out who saw her last and what she was doing, that kind of thing. Tad gave me the names of some of Tabitha's housekeeping clients, her preferred grocery store, her bank. And he said she goes to the library a lot."

DeeDee swiped at her phone screen over and over, shaking her head. "This is unbelievable. Tabitha has zero online presence. Same for her son. You'll have to ask him to e-mail you a picture of his mom."

"I'll do that right now." Jessica reached into her pocket for her own phone.

"Which deputy did Tad talk to?" Mary asked.

"Tom McGregor," Jessica answered.

"Did he at least agree to issue a BOLO for Tabitha's car?" Kaylee asked.

"Yes." Jessica hit send on her text and tucked the phone back into her apron pocket. "Tad did mention that."

A warm, familiar male voice entered their conversation. "Are you talking about last night's prowler at the Newton estate?"

Kaylee smiled at Reese Holt, who was channeling his usual laid-back vibe in worn jeans and a flannel shirt. He held a steaming cup of coffee in one hand and a brownie in the other.

"No," Jessica said, "the mother of a—"

"Yes, actually," Kaylee interjected. "It might be connected."

The color drained from Jessica's face. "A prowler? But you were in Tabitha's house. You told Tad there was no sign of foul play."

"There wasn't." Kaylee gestured for Reese to join them, then brought him up to speed on Tabitha's apparent disappearance and filled the women in on what she knew about the prowler incident at Pennybrook Grove.

"So the guy I saw escorting you across the yard was NSA?" Reese repeated, the incredulousness in his voice an odd mixture of relief and uncertainty. "They had a guy, Shawn, watching me the whole time I was working on the window, but he said he was the admiral's aide."

"A dark-haired linebacker kind of guy?" Kaylee asked, picturing the one who'd taken her down.

"No, that sounds like Mark, the other security guy," Reese said. "I guess he's probably NSA too, like your friend. Shawn is a gangly guy with thinning hair and square black glasses. I think you could take him if you had to." Reese winked, sparking a flutter in Kaylee's middle.

"Back to this prowler," Mary said. "He actually succeeded in getting into the house? Did he get away with anything?"

"They didn't say and I didn't ask," Reese answered.

Kaylee sighed. "I *did* ask, but they still didn't say."

"I didn't notice any other damage from where I was working," Reese went on. "But what I did notice was a decided chill in the air between the admiral and his wife. The admiral doesn't seem to get along with his son that well either."

DeeDee extended her fingers one at a time, as she named each person Reese had mentioned. "So we've got the admiral, his wife and son, his aide, and two NSA agents? Six people living or working on the property and I still couldn't get in touch with anyone? I mean, sure the driveway's gated, but—"

"Don't feel bad." Reese shook his head. "I got the impression only the son had been staying there until a few days ago when the admiral and his aide arrived. The wife only got in last night. And unfortunately for her, she's the one who surprised the prowler."

"How terrible," Kaylee said, then furrowed her brow. "Did the agents come with the admiral, or did they come after the prowler incident?"

"It seemed to me that they arrived this morning," Reese said. "One of them mentioned not getting any sleep on the plane."

Deputy Alan Brooks sidled up to the table, where his tall

frame loomed over them. "Did I hear you say the admiral flew in special agents to investigate their prowler incident?"

"Seems so," Reese said. "Do you know anything about it?"

Alan nodded his shaved head. "Yeah, I answered the alarm call last night. The admiral acted as if it was of little concern. He said it was probably just kids. And since nothing was taken, he didn't want us to waste our time trying to track them down."

"Did you happen to notice if the lights were on at the house next door when you drove past?" Kaylee asked.

Alan raised an eyebrow but answered anyway. "No, but I did pass a dark sedan as I was getting close to the estate. It wasn't speeding, and I didn't notice if it had come out of the admiral's property, but I wondered afterward if it might've been their prowler making a getaway. My first priority, of course, was to ensure no one was injured."

"Did your dashcam pick up the license plate number?" Mary asked.

Alan winced. "I hadn't flicked it on yet. Why were you asking about the house next door, Kaylee?"

"Tabitha Mason lives there," Kaylee said.

"A BOLO for her license plate came over the radio a half hour ago. She drives a dark-green Ford. That could've been the car I saw." A call came over the radio on the deputy's shoulder. He listened and radioed back that he was on his way. "Sorry, I've got to go."

"I don't like this at all," Jessica said as Alan rushed out of the bakery. "The admiral is clearly taking the intrusion far more seriously than he let on to Alan. What if Tabitha saw the intruder and he . . . ?" She let the thought trail off as if it were too awful to voice.

"There was no evidence of a struggle at Tabitha's house," Kaylee reminded her with a confidence she didn't feel. What if the intruder had forced Tabitha to drive him somewhere in her car and then silenced her?

Mary's thoughts must have veered in the same direction. "Did anyone find an abandoned vehicle near the estate?"

"Not that Phil mentioned," Kaylee said. "I think I'll have to have another chat with him."

Reese frowned. "This sounds like a case better left to the sheriff's department."

"Maybe," Jessica said. "But they've already made it clear to Tad that finding Tabitha isn't a priority."

Kaylee suddenly felt a heaviness weighing on her limbs. If the sheriff's department wasn't going to take Tabitha's odd disappearance seriously, somebody should. And considering her own involvement in the case so far, it appeared as though the task would fall to Kaylee, whether she liked it or not.

4

Friday afternoons were usually one of the flower shop's busiest times for walk-in customers, whether they were men eager to surprise their wives or evening dates with a romantic bouquet of roses, office workers celebrating payday with a bouquet for their dining room table, or dinner party guests picking up a hostess gift. But in the hour since Kaylee and Mary had returned to the shop, the shop's sole client was a young woman who bought some of DeeDee's handcrafted soap for a friend's birthday.

As Kaylee rang up the order, she said to Mary, "You might as well take the rest of the afternoon off. You could visit some of the places Tad thought his mom might've been recently. See what you can learn."

"It's Mallory, right?" Mary said to the customer. "You're a teller at Civic Trust Bank, aren't you?"

The young lady nodded. "That's right."

"Do you remember the last time Tabitha Mason was in?" Mary continued.

"Sure, I saw her yesterday morning."

"Did she mention if she was going anywhere?" Kaylee asked.

"Oh, I don't know." The teller shrugged. "I didn't help her. Naomi did."

"Naomi didn't happen to mention Tabitha making a large withdrawal yesterday, did she?" Mary pressed.

"Excuse me?" Mallory clutched the handle on her bag of soap and backed away from the counter.

"Wait," Kaylee said. "Sorry, we didn't mean to seem overbearing. It's just that Tabitha is missing and her son is very worried, but the sheriff won't investigate because he says she probably went on a trip. We're just trying to figure out if he could be right, to set her son's worries at ease."

"Oh." Mallory's grip relaxed slightly. "I guess I could ask around for you."

"That would be wonderful. Thank you." Kaylee handed Mallory the shop's business card. "You can call me here to let me know if you think Tad doesn't need to worry."

"Tad was always nice to me in high school," Mallory said as she accepted the card. "I hope nothing happened to his mom." With a nervous wave, the bank teller left the flower shop.

Mary chuckled as the door jingled closed behind Mallory. "I think I'd better stay here and let you go sweet-talk the grocer and librarian into spilling their guts. You clearly have a gift for spinning the question just right."

"You're sure you don't mind?" Kaylee asked.

"Not a bit. But I'd like to go with you to Tabitha's house tonight when you check on the cat. I don't want you going alone if something bad happened there."

"Sure. I'd appreciate the company." Kaylee glanced down at Bear, who was snoozing on a cushion nearby. "Be good, Bear. I'll be back by five."

Kaylee stopped in at the grocery store first. The girl at the cash register had no idea who Tabitha Mason was. Remembering the steak marinating in Tabitha's refrigerator, Kaylee went to the back of the store to ask the butcher. The woman behind the counter was busy serving a customer, but a young man in an apron must've noticed Kaylee waiting, because he came out through the swinging door from the back room. "May I help you?" he asked.

"I have a bit of an odd question," Kaylee answered. "Do you happen to know a woman named Tabitha Mason?"

His eyes twinkled. "She buys a T-bone steak every week. Two when her son is home from college."

"She had a steak that was packaged yesterday in her refrigerator. Do you remember when she came in?"

"Why? Was something wrong with the meat?"

"No, no, nothing like that," Kaylee reassured him. "She seems to have disappeared and we're trying to retrace her steps."

Concern rippled the man's brow. "That's terrible. She was here before noon yesterday."

"And did she mention any special plans? A trip off the island maybe?"

The man shrugged. "Women talk to me about meat. That's all. You ought to try her hairdresser. She looked as if she'd just had her hair cut."

"I'll do that. Thanks for your help."

With three salons in town and several more hairdressers working from their homes, finding Tabitha's hairdresser might be a challenge. However, considering Tabitha had had her hair done and then gone to the grocery store, Kaylee thought that the salon across the street was the best place to start her search, so she hurried over.

As Kaylee reached for the salon's door handle, the sound of a thick Bostonian accent drew her attention to the street corner, where two men were talking. The second man had a nasally voice, thinning red hair, and square-framed glasses. "Shawn?" Kaylee murmured to herself, recognizing him from Reese's description.

Only she must've said his name a little louder than she'd realized, because the man glanced her way. She quickly ducked inside the salon before he could ask her how she knew who he was.

The salon was crowded, not unexpected for a Friday afternoon. The stylist nearest the counter paused in the middle of her cutting job and approached the desk, where she flipped over a couple of pages in the appointment book. "The earliest available appointment we have is Monday at ten," she told Kaylee.

"Actually," Kaylee said, "I was wondering if Tabitha Mason gets her hair done here."

The woman hitched her thumb toward a young stylist at the far end of the long bank of mirrored counters. "Talk to Star." Star's hair was tipped with bright violet, no doubt a point on the plus side to Tad's purple-loving mom.

Kaylee made her way down the narrow room, earning a few curious glances from other stylists. She introduced herself to Star and asked about Tabitha's last visit.

"Yeah, she was here yesterday morning," Star said as she continued to roll curlers into her client's hair. "She told me her birthday was coming up and she wanted to go a little crazy, so we put a few highlights in. I couldn't convince her to go with purple though, even though she loves the color."

"Did she mention any trips she was taking?"

"Nope," Star answered. "And it didn't sound like she had much of a plan for her birthday at all, if you can believe it."

"Thanks for your help," Kaylee said, glancing around at the other customers and stylists. No one seemed to be curious about their conversation, yet she still had the feeling she was being watched. She returned to the front of the salon and spotted the admiral's aide loitering outside the picture window. He abruptly averted his gaze, and by the time she pushed through the door, he was gone.

Kaylee tried a few more of Tabitha's haunts with a similar lack of success, then rejoined Mary at The Flower Patch. Bear scurried across the gleaming floor toward her, his paws slipping back half the distance they gained on each stride. Kaylee laughed. "Nothing frustrates Bear more than when you polish the floor."

Mary shrugged. "It was that or rearrange the workroom."

"Did you hear back from Mallory?"

"Yes, she said Tabitha made a deposit, not a withdrawal."

Kaylee sighed. "That clinches it. There's nothing in her actions or conversations in the twenty-four hours before she disappeared to suggest she was planning to go away."

Mary flipped the sign in the window to *Closed* and locked the front door. "Let's go back to her house and see what clues we can turn up. You never know what we'll find."

Kaylee parked behind Mary's car in Tabitha's driveway and then climbed out with Bear on his leash. "I wonder if Phil finished gathering evidence," she said as Mary joined her. "I was going to let Bear snoop around in the fenced backyard while we look in on the cat, but maybe I'd better not."

Instead, Kaylee kept Bear on the leash while she led Mary around to the back, took a moment to confirm Tabitha's car hadn't reappeared in the garage, then showed Mary where they thought the prowler had jumped the fence.

Mary pointed to a clump of white plaster. "Looks as if your NSA friend has already made a cast of the prints, so I'm sure he's also gathered whatever other evidence he could."

Bear pranced in a joyful circle as if he understood that meant he'd get to explore.

Kaylee unclipped his leash. "Okay, boy, see if you can find us any clues." Bear immediately nosed the shrub Tabitha's cat had crouched under earlier, and Kaylee chuckled. "I guess he's more interested in finding Peony."

After retrieving the key from the frog, Kaylee let herself and Mary into the house, leaving Bear to sniff around the enclosed yard. Peony immediately came running from the direction of the front room and twined around Kaylee's legs. "Somebody's ready for supper."

The cat moved on to rub against Mary's legs next, leaving a thick sheen of ginger and white fur on her black slacks.

Mary groaned. "It's a good thing you're cute, Peony. You're shedding like crazy. Lily will never forgive me when she finds out I was with another cat." Lily was the little calico Mary's husband, Herb, had adopted, and she had completely stolen her family's hearts.

Kaylee poured fresh food and water in the cat's dish while Mary looked around. When Kaylee joined her in the front room, the coaster sat on the right-hand side of Tabitha's desk. "Did you move the coaster?" Kaylee pointed to it.

Mary shook her head. "No. Why?"

"It was on the left-hand side of the blotter this morning. I remember because it made me think Tabitha might be left-handed."

"Your NSA friend probably came in again."

Kaylee frowned. He knew where the key was, but he didn't have Tad's permission or a search warrant, at least as far as she knew. Without either of those things, the rule-abiding agent was unlikely to re-enter the home.

And if he had, why would he?

A wary feeling balled in the pit of her stomach. Phil couldn't think Tabitha had anything to do with the break-in, so did he know more about the prowler and Tabitha's possible fate than he'd admitted?

Mary's voice cut into Kaylee's thoughts. "Although you'd think a professional would be more careful about leaving everything the way he found it." With a shrug, Mary asked, "Should we check the bedrooms?"

"Sure," Kaylee said, then followed Mary down the hall and into Tabitha's bedroom.

"That's funny. Tabitha keeps her laptop in her bedroom instead of on the desk." Mary pointed to the bottom shelf of the nightstand, where a sleek silver laptop gleamed in the shadows. "I'll see if Jess wants to ask Tad if he knows the password. Tabitha might have a calendar on her computer that'd give us a clue to her plans."

"Good idea. I have Tad's number, but maybe it's better if the request comes from someone he's known longer."

While Mary typed her message to Jessica, Kaylee did another sweep of the master bedroom. She noticed that the wedding photo on the dresser had also been moved and the closet left open. The house had definitely been searched. She mentioned these changes to Mary.

"Maybe Deputy McGregor went through the place after Tad's call," Mary suggested.

"Could be." Either way, Kaylee wanted to know. Because if it wasn't a deputy or Phil, who was it? And what were they looking for?

She dialed the sheriff's station, and Aida Friedman, the receptionist, picked up on the first ring. She was a regular customer of The Flower Patch and had interacted with Kaylee on several other cases, so they were on friendly terms. "Hi, Aida," Kaylee said. "It's Kaylee. I was wondering if you could answer a few questions for me."

"Let me guess—you're calling about Tabitha Mason," Aida responded, and Kaylee could hear her smiling on the other end of the line. "You know, grown women are allowed to take spontaneous trips."

"Yes, they certainly are," Kaylee said. "But her son is worried. He asked me to check Tabitha's house again, and I'm here right now. Can you tell me if any deputies have been by today?"

"We didn't send anyone out there. The office has been

swamped with calls all day. We haven't had an officer to spare."

"Thanks, Aida." Kaylee said goodbye, then pocketed her phone. She told Mary what Aida had said, then added, "I'm going to drive over to Pennybrook Grove and see if I can talk to Phil."

"I'll wait here to see if Jessica can get hold of Tad," Mary answered. "Good luck."

"Thanks, I might need it."

Kaylee wasn't exactly sure how she'd get anyone's attention if the gate was still locked, since there didn't seem to be a call button or intercom, but she'd think of something. *If all else fails, I know vaulting the fence will bring a quick response.* She rubbed her hip, which was still sore from that morning's surprise takedown. Going over the fence again probably wasn't such a good idea.

Leaving Bear in the yard, where he was happily basking in the sunshine, Kaylee drove down the street and parked in front of the Newtons' entrance, then climbed out and rattled the gate. Sure enough, it was still locked tight, so Kaylee returned to the car and honked her horn, waited a couple of minutes, then hit it again.

On her fifth attempt, Phil joined her at the gate. "I guess I should've given you my cell phone number," he said, then pulled out his phone and the business card she'd given him. He tapped the screen for a few seconds, and then Kaylee's phone buzzed with an incoming text. "That's from me so you have my number. What's up?"

"I saw that you returned to Tabitha's and took casts of the footprints," Kaylee said. "Did you go back inside the house?"

"I didn't have a search warrant."

Not missing the fact that he hadn't actually answered the question, Kaylee glanced at his slacks. They were pristine, without a speck of cat hair on them. He could've brushed them clean or changed into a fresh pair, but for the moment, it didn't appear that he'd had a run-in with Peony. "So you didn't go inside?"

"Why? Did you find something I should know about?"

Kaylee narrowed her eyes. "Do you make a habit of answering questions with questions?"

He chuckled. "Sorry. It's the nature of my work."

"When did you get to the island?" Kaylee asked.

"I came in on the early ferry this morning."

"So you don't normally travel with the admiral?"

"No. I fly wherever I'm needed. Two weeks ago, I was in Alaska. Next week I might be in New York."

"So you came here because of the prowler?" Kaylee decided not to let on she knew the admiral had declined to involve the sheriff's department in the investigation.

"That's right."

"But the admiral has been here for a while?"

"A few days. He's taking a month's leave before he starts his new assignment."

The admiral's aide, Shawn, pulled up his car behind Kaylee's and stuck his head out the window. "Are you going in?"

"No, sorry," Kaylee said, realizing her SUV was blocking the gate. "I'll move out of your way."

She pulled off to the side, where Phil stood waiting for her. The aide shot Phil a scathing glance as he drove past.

"He doesn't appear to be too happy with you," Kaylee said, rejoining Phil.

The muscle in his jaw twitched. "His job is to be protective of the admiral's privacy. He's probably concerned my fraternizing with a pretty brunette could lead to a security breach."

Kaylee's heart did a silly flip at the compliment.

A sporty red car roared down the one-lane driveway from the house and crunched to a halt on the gravel just before it would have smashed into Shawn's modest sedan. Ryan jumped out of the sports car at the same time the admiral's wife climbed out of the back seat of the sedan.

"Where are you off to now?" Diane asked in a clipped tone.

Kaylee couldn't hear Ryan's response, but it must've met with Diane's satisfaction, because she handed him some money and gave him a hug. As she turned to climb back into the aide's car, Kaylee's heart did a second flip. A mass of cat hairs clung to the cuffs of the woman's dark slacks.

"Do the Newtons have a pet?" Kaylee asked Phil.

"No. Why?"

Kaylee shrugged, hoping it looked nonchalant. "Just curious." But was it a coincidence?

Diane could be returning from visiting someone with a pet. After all, why would she search Tabitha's house? Let alone know where to find the key?

Unless she'd spied on Kaylee and Phil this morning when they'd returned it to its hiding spot.

Kaylee frowned as she watched Shawn's sedan meander away up the driveway toward the mansion. She couldn't help but feel as if Diane Newton was hiding something.

5

Kaylee left Phil at Pennybrook Grove and returned to Tabitha's. She parked once again behind Mary's car, which made her realize something. If either Mrs. Newton or the admiral's aide had been the ones to search Tabitha's house earlier, seeing Mary's car there as they passed a moment ago must've roused some curiosity.

"I wish I could take this cat home with me until Tabitha turns up," Mary said, coming out of the back door with the calico nestled in her arms. "It'd save having to send someone around here every day to feed her. I don't think Lily would react well to my bringing a second cat in the house, though. Her buddy Bear is one thing, but a rival kitty is another."

"I think Peony might feel more comfortable here anyway," Kaylee said, joining Mary on the stoop. "Don't you?"

"I'm not so sure. She likes attention." Mary scratched the cat's chin, eliciting a loud purr as if to prove her point.

"Her being here gives us a good excuse to check in every day. Maybe keep an eye on what's going on next door." Kaylee told Mary about the cat hair on Diane's slacks. "My gut tells me they know more about their prowler than they're letting on, and maybe more about Tabitha's disappearance too."

"Wouldn't your friend tell you if he had information that could help us locate her?"

Kaylee failed to conceal her wince. "I'd like to think so. But Phil's first loyalty is to national security."

"The only security I can imagine finding Tabitha would jeopardize is the prowler's if she can identify him."

"Me too." Kaylee scratched the cat's ears, and her contented purring grew even louder.

Bear stood on his hind legs and pawed at Mary's knees, clearly wanting her to bring the potential playmate to his level.

The cat tensed and tried to crawl higher up Mary's arms.

"Sorry, Bear. You make her nervous," Mary said.

"Did you ever hear back from Jessica about Tad and the password for Tabitha's computer?" Kaylee asked.

Mary shook her head. "No, and it's getting late. We probably ought to head out. But I think you should at least keep the house key with you this time to stop anyone else from sneaking in."

"Good plan." Kaylee slid the key into her pocket, then frowned at the Newtons' property. "This whole situation doesn't make sense. The admiral told Deputy Brooks the prowler didn't steal anything, so why would he escalate potential charges by kidnapping Tabitha or silencing her or whatever? He wouldn't, right? But if she just got scared after seeing the prowler and went into hiding, why wouldn't she tell her son?"

"Maybe the admiral lied about nothing being stolen," Mary said.

"Maybe," Kaylee agreed grimly. And if he hadn't told the truth about that, how many other falsehoods were swirling over at Pennybrook Grove?

The next afternoon, DeeDee and her girls, Reese, and Sara met Kaylee and Bear outside the lighthouse keeper's quarters for camp registration.

Sara set a box filled with various potted plants down beside a stack of clear empty pots and stayed at ground level to pet Bear.

"Don't you look especially handsome today." She admired the green polka-dot bow tie Kaylee had put on him for the occasion.

"For those who know Bear from The Flower Patch, his bow ties are kind of his trademark," Kaylee explained. "I figured the kids would like the dots."

Sara nodded. "I have a student named Ellie who gets nervous around dogs, but she loves polka dots. Hopefully if she comes out, the bow tie will make him not seem so scary to her."

Kaylee frowned. "I never considered that some of the children might not feel comfortable around a dog. Maybe I should—"

"Don't sweat it," DeeDee interjected. "He's so small and friendly. He'll be fine. I've never seen him frighten anyone."

"Oh, yes. I'm sure it'll be fine." Sara rummaged through the box she'd brought and pulled out a handful of colorful index cards. "I'd better set these around the grounds before the children start arriving."

While Sara set up the plant-related mystery activity she'd masterminded to give the children a taste of the fun to come in the week ahead, Reese hung the big welcome banner they'd made.

DeeDee showed Kaylee a couple of age-appropriate mystery books. "I found these plant-themed mysteries and thought we could use them as prizes for some activity or awards at the end."

Kaylee thumbed through one. "That's a great idea. Even reluctant readers seem to enjoy a good mystery. We can display them on the registration table."

As Kaylee and DeeDee arranged the table, they talked about what little new information they'd gathered about Tabitha's activities prior to her disappearance.

"I don't know what more we can do to try to find her," Kaylee said.

"Me neither," DeeDee replied. "But Jessica is beside herself with worry for poor Tad. She always had a soft spot for the boy. I think it broke her heart more than Mila's when they broke up before college. But they were studying on opposite sides of the country."

"Long-distance relationships are tough," Kaylee murmured, not that she was speaking from experience. Romantic relationships had never been her forte. She'd always been too invested in her studies and then later her job. She glanced at Reese and wondered if their relationship might one day blossom beyond good friends. Now that she'd been on Orcas Island for a while and learned not to take life so seriously, she might actually be ready. But was Reese? She could count on one hand the number of times she'd heard him mention his former fiancée. Was that because he was over the heartbreak? Or because it was still too painful to talk about? And even if he was ready to move on, would he be interested in her?

"Everything's ready," DeeDee said, breaking into Kaylee's musings. "Let's brainstorm more ideas on how to track down Tabitha while we wait for the kids to arrive."

Before Kaylee could say "good idea," however, the first van load of campers pulled into the parking lot.

Sara scurried to the registration table. "The cards and plants are all set out over there." She motioned to the open area behind and to the side of the keeper's quarters, where potted plants related to the clues on the cards dotted the landscape, then held up a stack of yellow cards. "Give each child one of these when he or she registers and it will get them started."

Reese climbed down from his ladder, the banner in place. "Anything else I can do to help?"

"Sure, if you really want to get involved." Sara grinned. "You can help any children struggling to decipher the clues, especially the younger ones. I want the activity to be challenging, but not so challenging it isn't fun anymore."

Reese read a card containing the first clue. "'These spring

flowers grow from bulbs from Holland. They grow in a variety of colors, but red is the most famous, which happens to be the same color as something on your face that shares part of its name.'" He chuckled, then scanned the yard. "Got it. If none of the clues are harder than this, I can handle it. Otherwise, we might have to consult the plant expert over here." He gestured casually toward Kaylee.

The yard was soon filled with laughing children scurrying from one clue to the next while their parents watched from the sidelines. When they finished the mystery game, kids moved on to the three activity stations that had also been set up. One was completing a jigsaw puzzle by cutting out the shapes on the back of the clue cards they'd collected to that point. It directed them back to the registration table to select one of the small clear pots from Sara's box. Then off they went again to decorate it at the second station, and finally, at the last stop, fill it with dirt and plant a marigold seed inside that would hopefully sprout before the end of the camp.

Kaylee was helping kids select their pots at the registration table when Phil drove in and nodded to her. Once parked, he stood next to his dark-blue truck and surveyed the action on the field.

Reese must have noticed his arrival too, because he walked over and talked to him.

Phil's gaze drifted to where Kaylee sat. She waved and he sauntered over. Reese started in beside him, but was sidetracked by a summoning from Sara.

"I saw the sign from the road," Phil said in greeting. "I thought I'd come in to see how many kids will be on Monday's field trip."

"We have over thirty children registered so far," Kaylee said. "It might seem like a lot more right now because the parents are hanging around and we said that younger siblings could tag along for today's activity."

Phil surveyed the scene once more. "Looks like they're having a blast. So what time should we expect you Monday?"

"Camp is only half days, in the afternoons. Is one o'clock okay?"

Phil nodded. "No problem. I'll be sure the gate is open for you."

Kaylee chuckled. "I'd appreciate that."

"This reminds me of the camp you and my sister volunteered at the summer after your freshman year." He grinned. "Remember the boat races down the river the two of you somehow convinced me to help with?"

"And one little boy's boat got stuck in an eddy in the middle of the creek and you waded in to free it."

"And ended up flat on my face in the water."

Kaylee laughed at the memory. "I promise we won't be having any boat races at Pennybrook Grove."

"Glad to hear it." Phil gazed kindly down at a little gap-toothed girl who was crouched next to the table making a fuss over Bear. "You like dogs?"

She shook her head. "No."

Bear responded with a sloppy kiss across her cheek, earning him a hug from the youngster.

"No, huh? Could have fooled me." Phil chuckled. "What's your friend's name?"

"Teacher said he's Bear, like my teddy bear."

"I see." Phil crouched next to her and scratched behind Bear's ears. "And what's your name?"

"I'm Ellie. I'm seven," she said proudly.

Kaylee's eyebrows went up. Was this the Ellie who was afraid of dogs? It would explain why Sara would compare Bear to a teddy bear to ease the girl's nervousness.

"Ellie," a woman called, "are you going to decorate your pot?"

The girl snatched a pot from the nearby box and sprang to her feet. "Excuse me. I have to go."

Phil stood, grinning as he fixed his attention on Kaylee. "Well, if the rest of your campers are half as sweet and polite as that one, it'll be a pleasure to have them visit the estate."

"We'll do our best to ensure they all behave."

Soon after Phil drove off, a young boy raced over to the registration table for a pot, but something else on the ground caught his attention and he bent to pick it up.

"What have you found there?" Kaylee asked.

"A clue," the youngster declared.

"May I see it?"

He held up a matchbook from Golightly's, the closest thing to a nightclub Turtle Cove could boast.

"Sweetie, that's not a clue." Kaylee reached for the matchbook. "May I have it?"

"No." He snapped his arm behind his back. "It's mine. I found it. It's a clue."

"How about we ask Ms. Wright if it's a clue? You know Ms. Wright from school?"

The boy nodded.

"Well, she organized this activity. So she'll know if the matchbook is a clue. Okay?"

The boy looked at the dirt and scuffed at it with his toe. "I guess."

Kaylee waved Sara over. Reese trailed Sara to the table with a curious expression.

"Could you tell us if the matchbook this boy found is a clue in your game?" Kaylee asked.

After the boy reluctantly showed Sara the matchbook, she frowned and shook her head. "I'm sorry, Caleb. That's not a clue, and you need to give it to me."

"No! I found it. Finders keepers."

"I'm afraid I can't let you keep it," Sara said firmly. "Matches are dangerous."

The boy's hand clamped tighter around the matchbook.

"If you want to keep them, you could give them to your dad to hold for you," Kaylee suggested.

The boy's face blanched so fast, Kaylee had to swallow a chuckle.

"Did I hear you say you found a matchbook?" Reese asked.

The boy's eyes widened as his gaze stretched up to meet Reese's. "Uh, yeah."

"Because I lost mine. Can I trade you something for the one you found?" He reached into his pocket and produced a quarter. "Would this be a fair trade?"

"Sure!" The boy swiped the quarter and replaced it with the matchbook as fast as he could. "Thanks," he said and ran off twenty-five cents richer.

"You forgot your pot," Sara called after him. She picked it up and strode off to deliver it to him.

"I'm impressed," Kaylee said to Reese. "Do you have a degree in child psychology I don't know about?"

Reese's eyes sparkled. "Nope. I just remember what worked on me as a kid." He flipped open the cover of the matchbook. "Besides, it's always handy to have a matchbook on you." He shook his head. "But whoever lost these might be kicking himself. He lost someone's phone number." He turned it around and showed Kaylee a phone number written inside.

Kaylee shrugged. "Too bad, I guess."

Reese's expression lost a touch of its sparkle and, after a beat, he asked, "What did your NSA friend want?"

"He needed to know what time to expect us Monday so he could make sure the gate was unlocked," Kaylee explained.

"He couldn't just call?" Reese's tone didn't quite sound like his usual easygoing self.

"He was curious about what kind of campers they could expect. And I think he was relieved to see they are all fairly amiable youngsters."

Reese nodded. "I spoke to the admiral only briefly, but it's hard to imagine he'd be keen on having a group of children traipsing through his yard. Your friend must have quite an influence on him."

Kaylee tilted her head at the edge Reese's voice had when he said the word "friend." He seemed to dislike Phil for some reason. And she'd never known Reese to dislike anyone. "I think Phil felt bad about the way his colleague tackled me when I breached their perimeter and wanted to make it up to me—being his kid sister's best friend in college and all."

"Huh," Reese said, not sounding convinced.

Kaylee shifted her focus to the families starting to drift back to their cars. "See you Monday," she said to the students as they passed.

Sara carried over a box of dirt-filled, child-decorated pots. "Can I store these inside the cottage?"

"Sure," Kaylee said. "It's still open."

Sara deposited her box inside the keeper's quarters, then came back outside to help Kaylee, Reese, and DeeDee take down the registration table and gather the clues and potted plants from the mystery game.

Reese, DeeDee, and Sara were packing supplies in Sara's car and Kaylee was locking up the keeper's quarters when a sheriff's deputy cruiser drove in.

Deputy Brooks pulled up beside her and rolled down his window. "I thought you might like to know we found your friend's car."

Kaylee's pulse jumped. "Tabitha's? Where?"

"In the parking lot at the ferry dock. Should've been the first place we looked, but the day her son phoned in the missing person's report was crazy with one call after another. Anyway, it seems to support the sheriff's opinion that Mrs. Mason simply took a trip off island without telling her son."

Kaylee shook her head, thinking of Tabitha's forgotten cat and the marinating steak left in her refrigerator. *Or that's what someone wants us to believe.*

6

Kaylee's expression must've given away her fears because DeeDee and Reese rushed over to her the instant Alan drove off.

"What is it?" DeeDee asked. "Did they find Tabitha?"

"No, they found her car," Kaylee answered. "She left it at the ferry dock. Or at least someone did."

Sara joined them, her forehead furrowed. "Did you say Tabitha, as in Tabitha Mason?"

"You know her? Do you know where she is?" Hope seeped back into Kaylee's chilled limbs.

"I don't know where she is at the moment. I didn't realize she was missing." Sara pulled out her phone and tapped on it, then raised the phone to her ear. After a moment she frowned and lowered it again. "That's weird. It usually goes to her voice mail if she doesn't pick up."

"When's the last time you saw her?" Kaylee asked.

"Thursday night," Sara replied. "It's part of why I was late for the meeting here."

DeeDee frowned in confusion. "What do you mean? I thought you had a volleyball game."

"She called me when I was on my way from the game to the meeting and said she was supposed to meet a guy at The Sunfish Café. She'd been corresponding with him online but had only met him in person once, so she was kind of nervous. You know how it is. Anyway, she asked me to stop by the café so I could 'rescue' her from the date, if need be."

Kaylee shifted Bear's leash from one hand to the other. "Can you describe this guy?"

Sara shook her head. "No. I never actually saw them together. I caught up to Tabitha on the street before she was supposed to meet him. She didn't want us to walk into the café together, in case he was already there. And he must've been."

"What do you mean?" DeeDee asked.

"Well, I was going to walk around the block a little and enter the café alone. We'd worked out a signal Tabitha would give me if I was supposed to interrupt the date." Sara sighed. "But by the time I got there, there was no sign of her. I figured they'd come and gone, maybe to a different restaurant. I waited around for a while, then I texted Tabitha to ask if everything was okay. She texted back, 'Great. Thanks.' I assumed they'd decided to go somewhere nicer for dinner, so I headed over to the meeting."

"Thinking she was fine," Kaylee added quietly.

"She said she was." Sara sounded a tad defensive. "If her car's still at the ferry dock, maybe they took a trip to the mainland together. Although that's not like her at all." She shook her head, suddenly much more distraught. "Some friend I am. I should've called later that night to ask about the date, but I was so busy prepping the game for today I never gave her another thought."

"It's not your fault," DeeDee reassured her.

Sara fiddled with her phone, flipping it over and over in her hand. "I guess somewhere in the back of my mind I figured she would eventually call to give me the scoop on her date. But I should've followed up. I've always worried about these online meets. The guys often seem way too good to be true."

"Did she mention her date's name?" Kaylee asked.

Sara's gaze drifted as she seemed to search her memory banks. "She must have, but I can't remember it."

"Well, please let me know right away if it comes to you," Kaylee said.

"Absolutely." Sara meandered off to her car, looking a lot

less cheerful than she'd been when the children were there.

"And then you'll give his name straight to Alan, right?" Reese's voice was firm, making his words sound like they weren't a suggestion.

"Of course." She really should tell the deputy, even if it hadn't been her original instinct.

Bear started to pull on his leash, so Kaylee started for her car too, but DeeDee caught her arm. "We should update Jessica and Mary and decide what we can do with this new information."

Kaylee nodded. "I agree. I need to stop by the flower shop and help Mary close up, but after that we can meet you at Death by Chocolate."

"I'm in too," Reese volunteered. "I don't want you getting into trouble without me."

Half an hour later, Kaylee and Mary left Bear napping on his bed in The Flower Patch and caught up with the other Petal Pushers and Reese next door. Jessica poured them each a hot cup of coffee and set out a plate of decadent treats.

"I can't believe Tad didn't mention his mom was meeting men online," Jessica said as she handed out dessert plates and napkins.

"I can." DeeDee selected a chocolate shortbread cookie and set it on her plate. "Dating is probably tricky for a widowed parent on a small island, even if the kids are grown up."

"Online dating can be so dangerous," Mary said. "You never really know who is on the other end."

Jessica retrieved her cell phone from her apron. "I'm going to call Tad to check in. I can ask if he knows anything about the date."

"Did he know his mom's password?" Kaylee asked.

"He said he'd think about it, but he hasn't gotten back to me," Jessica answered as she dialed. "He did e-mail me a photo, though, and I forwarded it to you, Kaylee."

"If Tabitha is anything like my mom, her password could be as easy as the word 'password.'" Reese smirked, then took a sip of coffee.

DeeDee chuckled. "My mom did the same thing. She thought no one would ever think it was something so simple."

"He's not answering," Jessica reported, then left a message when the voice mail kicked in.

"We should visit the café," Mary suggested. "Perhaps the waitress will remember seeing Tabitha and her date."

Jessica asked Gretchen to take charge of closing the shop for the day while Kaylee retrieved Bear, then they all headed over to The Sunfish Café.

The classic, reasonably priced fare at the restaurant made it a popular spot for tourists and locals alike. As usual, the place was packed for dinner service.

Mary peered through the window. "Maybe only one or two of us should go in. How about you and Reese?" she asked Kaylee, taking Bear's leash from her.

"Works for me," Reese said. He opened the door and held it for Kaylee to enter first.

"There's an empty table in the back corner," the harried server said as she bustled past them, balancing a tray full of dirty dishes. "I'll be right with you."

"We actually aren't here to—" Kaylee cut off her explanation since the server had already pushed through the swinging kitchen door.

"We might as well sit down," Reese said. "The back corner will be a quieter place to ask her about Tabitha anyway."

They sat at the tiny, bare table, their knees bumping beneath it. Reese grinned. "Cozy."

The server burst through the swinging kitchen door carrying two sets of cutlery swaddled in clean napkins and snatched up two menus as she passed the cash register. Setting them on the table, she asked, "Can I get you a drink to start?"

Reese flashed her a warm smile that coaxed her to pause and take a breath. "We're sorry to bother you. We're actually hoping for some information about a friend's mother who's missing. Tabitha Mason. She was supposed to meet a date here Thursday night around six. Were you working then?"

"I was working, and I know Tabitha. But she didn't come in that night. Was that why Sara came in asking about her?" The woman suddenly sounded deeply concerned, and her face paled. "Do they think it was foul play?"

"There's no evidence to suggest that," Kaylee said quickly. "It appears she might've gone off island, but her son hasn't been able to reach her and is worried."

"Tad's a good kid. He worked as a busboy here when he was in high school." The server frowned. "I wish I could help you."

"Did you happen to notice a guy here who maybe seemed to be waiting for someone but then left without eating?" Kaylee asked.

The server thought for a moment, then nodded. "Yeah, now that you mention it, there was a guy. But he didn't come in until closer to seven. He ordered a coffee and watched the window and checked his phone a lot. I figured he'd already eaten and was killing time until the ferry left. He hung around until almost eight."

"Did he happen to mention whether he was waiting for someone?" Reese asked. "Or give his name?"

"No, he didn't talk much," the waitress answered.

Kaylee leaned forward. "Can you describe him?"

"We need the check over here!" a hefty man bellowed from

a table near the front of the café.

The server's harried expression returned. "The guy was about six foot. Short, dark hair." She squeezed her eyes shut for a moment, then opened them again and said, "He was wearing a pressed button-down shirt and black slacks, and he was carrying a yellow rain slicker."

"That's great." Reese handed her one of his business cards. "Give me a call if you think of anything else later. Thanks."

The server tucked the card into her apron, then hurried toward the impatient customer now repeating his demand for the check.

Reese left a generous tip on the table, then he and Kaylee joined the rest of the Petal Pushers outside.

"Any luck?" DeeDee asked.

"Tabitha never came in," Kaylee said. "The server remembers one guy hanging around as if he might've been waiting for someone, but he didn't come in until almost an hour later than the time Tabitha's date was supposed to meet her, so chances are he wasn't our guy." Kaylee relayed the server's description of the man, then gazed at Mary. "Come to think of it, he might be the same guy we almost hit after the meeting Thursday night. He was carrying a yellow slicker, and the time frame fits."

Jessica sighed. "If he wasn't with Tabitha, it doesn't help us. And I still haven't heard back from Tad, so maybe we should just go over to Tabitha's and see if we can crack her computer's password ourselves. If we can get her date's name, we might at least have a hope of tracking him down. And maybe he can lead us to her."

Mary craned her neck and squinted at the surveillance camera on the outside corner of the nearby bank. "Or we could ask the local business owners if we can look at their footage from around six o'clock Thursday evening." She pointed to another surveillance camera installed under the eaves above a drugstore's front door.

"One of these might've captured where Tabitha headed after she parked her car in the ferry lot."

"We won't be able to ask at the bank until Monday," Reese said. "It's closed for the weekend."

"Okay." Jessica scanned the eaves of all the nearby buildings. "But there are two cameras in the ferry port parking lot. Mary, DeeDee, and I can go ask to see the footage from those while Kaylee and Reese talk to the drugstore manager. We'll take Bear too since the ferry office is outside."

Kaylee had taken note of the way her friends kept pairing her off with Reese, and it was becoming embarrassingly obvious the choice wasn't random. She knew there was a time when she would have protested, but now . . . well, it felt nice to work side by side with Reese on an investigation.

Once inside the drugstore, Reese took the lead in asking the manager for permission to view his surveillance footage, while Kaylee purchased a couple of bags of chips and dog treats to tide them all over until dinner.

"I would let you," the balding, middle-aged manager was saying to Reese as Kaylee joined them, "but the other investigators already took the tapes."

Kaylee's brow furrowed. *Other investigators?*

"Thank you anyway," Reese said. Clasping Kaylee's elbow, he guided her back outside.

"The sheriff must've changed his mind about investigating Tabitha's disappearance," Kaylee said. "I'll call him right now to compare notes. He might not know about the date Tabitha was supposed to be meeting."

Sheriff Eddie Maddox picked up on the first ring, but when Kaylee asked him about the surveillance footage, he said, "Sorry, Kaylee. My deputies didn't collect those tapes. But I'd like to know who's posing as investigators around here." His tone told her he wasn't happy about the news.

After saying goodbye to Eddie, Kaylee relayed his response to Reese. "The 'investigators' must've been Phil and Mark," she said. She couldn't help but be miffed that Phil hadn't said anything when he stopped by the camp registration, when he must've already heard about Tabitha's car being found. In fact, that was likely why he'd really been in town—to check for surveillance footage.

"Easy enough to find out." Reese opened the drugstore's door and motioned Kaylee to go in ahead of him. "Were the investigators you spoke to in uniform?" he asked the manager.

"No, plain clothes."

"Did they give their names?"

The manager frowned. "No. They don't work with you?"

"No," Reese said. "Could you describe them?"

The manager gave two vague descriptions that loosely matched Phil and Mark.

Kaylee lit up with a revelation. "You must have them on today's security footage, from when they came in. Can we look at that?"

The manager's brow creased. "No, those guys didn't come in today. They came in first thing yesterday morning, as soon as I opened. If they were on the tape, it would've been on the same one I handed over to them."

Kaylee fumed. Clearly Phil knew more than he was telling her. And he had from the moment he'd arrived.

7

Kaylee and Jessica drove to Tabitha's house hoping to find the name of her date on her laptop. The cat sprang outside the instant Kaylee unlocked the back door.

"I guess she's not used to being cooped up inside all day," Jessica said.

"Good thing Bear decided to keep napping in the car or we could've had a chase on our hands." Kaylee watched as Peony dashed down the driveway to investigate a bush at the far end, then led Jessica inside. "I'll fill the cat's food and water dishes and clean her litter pan if you want to start trying to crack Tabitha's computer password. Her laptop is in the bedroom, but there's a desk in the front room you can use."

By the time Kaylee joined Jessica in the front room, Jessica appeared frustrated—and unsuccessful. "I've exhausted all the lame passwords I can think of," Jessica said. "And I couldn't find any notes in the desk that looked like they would be passwords."

Kaylee picked up a large family Bible sitting on the bookshelf. "Have you tried birth dates?"

"Just Tad's. His was the only one I knew."

Kaylee rattled off Tabitha's, then her late husband's, then their anniversary, his parents' anniversary, and so on, until they'd tried, in various combinations, every one listed except Tad's.

"Should we try mixing up Tad's month with his mom's day and his dad's year?" Kaylee asked. "Or some other similar combination?"

"It can't hurt. So 05 for May," Jessica said as she typed.

"Who's that for? None of them have a birthday in May."

"Tad's is May fifth."

"No, Tad's is March fifth," Kaylee said. "At least according to the Bible."

"Seriously? I can't believe I remembered that wrong." Jessica deleted what she'd already typed and began again. A few key strokes later, she let out a celebratory whoop. "We're in. Tad's actual birth date was the password."

While Kaylee watched over her shoulder, Jessica opened the computer's web browser and checked the saved bookmarks and browsing history.

"Either Tabitha is diligent about clearing her browsing history or she doesn't surf much." Jessica started typing in the web addresses of popular dating sites. "The address bar isn't auto-filling in the suggestions I'd expect either. It doesn't appear as if she frequented any dating site I've ever heard of."

"Want to check her e-mail?" Kaylee suggested.

"I think that's our next step. I didn't do that at first because a lot of the dating sites protect users' privacy by enabling them to private message within the site," Jessica explained.

"How do you know so much about dating sites?" Kaylee asked teasingly. "You're a married woman."

"I have a twenty-six-year-old unmarried daughter who likes to talk about her love life with her mother." Jessica clicked on an envelope icon on the toolbar, but Tabitha's mail program opened to an empty in-box. "She must use an online mail program."

"Or she's as fastidious about keeping her mailbox as clutter free as the rest of her house." Kaylee gestured toward the bookshelves. "Her books are arranged in alphabetical order by author, like a library. The spice jars in the cupboard are arranged in alphabetical order. Everything you could think of has been catalogued and filed. There isn't a single unsorted catch-all dish, let alone drawer or closet where things merely get tossed."

"When we find her, I'm asking her for lessons," Jessica said with a quick grin, then reopened the Internet browser and tried typing addresses for popular e-mail programs in the search bar, but none of them auto-filled to indicate Tabitha's preferred program either. She paused, then peered at Kaylee thoughtfully. "What if whoever snuck in here after you yesterday erased any incriminating data from the computer?"

"Did you check the computer's trash bin?" Kaylee asked.

A few mouse clicks later, Jessica said, "Empty. Wait a second, let me try the one inside her e-mail program too." Jessica clicked on the deleted items button. "Ha! I think we've found our man."

Kaylee squinted at the e-mail, a copy of one sent by Tabitha Thursday evening at 5:47 p.m. to someone named Ned Banford.

"It confirms she'll meet this Ned guy at the café as proposed, but that she'll need to make it for seven," Jessica said. "This has got to be the date she called Sara about."

"But why'd she tell Sara six then?"

"Maybe she asked Sara before the time change." Jessica pointed to Tabitha's postscript. "Check this out—she warned him to bring his rain slicker because it was supposed to rain."

"So the time and the fact he was carrying a rain slicker fits with the guy at the Sunfish." Kaylee made a note of the man's name and e-mail address. "Maybe we can track him down and get some answers."

Jessica swiveled the office chair she was sitting in to face Kaylee. "But what if he's responsible for Tabitha's disappearance, and not because their date went well?"

Kaylee's heart dropped a beat at the same time she remembered her promise to Reese to be careful. "Once we locate him, we can ask the sheriff to question him."

"That's a good idea." Jessica's phone beeped with a text alert. Glancing at the screen, she said, "Sounds as if we've been wasting our time."

"What do you mean?"

"Tad just called off the search. He says he heard from his mom. She's visiting a sick aunt." Jessica tried to phone him back and frowned when it kept ringing. "That's annoying. He's not picking up."

"Maybe he has his ringer volume turned off." Kaylee frowned. "It seems weird, don't you think? I mean, if Tabitha left of her own free will, why didn't she ensure her cat was looked after?"

"Maybe it was a sudden thing," Jessica suggested. "It'd explain the abandoned steak—and the abandoned date."

"Even so, you'd think once she realized she wasn't going to be back within a day or so, she would've called her usual cat sitter to come in and check on Peony."

"That's true. No matter how sick the aunt was, it's hard to believe she'd totally forget about her cat." Jessica logged off of the computer. "Unless Tabitha met up with her date before reaching the café and was hesitant to admit to Tad she left the island with a virtual stranger, so she made up the sick aunt story." Jessica batted her eyelashes like a starlet who'd finally found her man, then shook her head. "That still doesn't explain why she'd neglect the cat. Unless maybe Peony had been missing for a few days and Tabitha thought she was gone. Cats do that, especially this time of year."

"Hmm." Kaylee still had an uneasy feeling about the whole thing, but maybe that was because she didn't like knowing Phil was keeping secrets from her. "At least we can assume Tabitha must be okay if she's talked to Tad."

"Yes. But I'd feel better if I could talk to *him*." Jessica's thumb hovered over her phone's screen as she debated trying him again. "It seems odd for him not to answer when I called within seconds of his text."

"He could've been at work or with friends or something and only able to text. It can be difficult to take a phone call without everyone around you noticing."

"I suppose."

"I think I remember seeing an address book in the desk. We could call his aunt's home to touch base with Tabitha," Kaylee suggested.

Jessica rolled her chair out a few inches and opened the center drawer, then retrieved a purple leather address book. "We don't know her last name," she said as she thumbed through the gold-edged pages. "Unless she's unmarried, it wouldn't be the same as Tabitha's maiden name. Did that family Bible you had out before list aunts and uncles?"

Kaylee retrieved the Bible once more and studied the family tree. "No, it doesn't."

Jessica went through the rest of the book. "I recognized all the female names in here as islanders except for three." She showed them to Kaylee. "Do you recognize these?"

"Nope."

They tried calling each in turn. One number was no longer in service, and the other two belonged to Tabitha's housekeeping clients.

At the sound of the cat scratching at the door and mewing, Kaylee went to let her in. Catching sight of a wall clock, she called back to Jessica, "We'd better call it a day. Luke is probably wondering if you're ever coming home."

Jessica glanced at her watch. "I'll say." She joined Kaylee at the back door, and they walked out together. "And I guess we need to abide by Tad's wishes. But I can't help feeling something still isn't right. You know what I mean?"

Kaylee locked the door behind them and then glanced toward the Newton estate and nodded. "I've got the same feeling."

"Well, it's just you and me tonight," Kaylee said to Bear as she turned the car toward home. "What do you say we pick up a pizza and then watch a movie? How does *Homeward Bound* sound?" Bear gave an answering bark that sounded like agreement, and Kaylee laughed. "I thought you'd approve."

She pulled to the side of the road and called in an order to The Right Slice. "We have some time to kill while they make it," she said to Bear as she pulled back onto the road. "I think I'll pop into the grocery store and grab some brownies." Sure, she knew she should be choosing a nice big salad or something healthy, but as hungry as she was, she just wanted comfort food. And it didn't help she was still a little—okay, maybe a lot—miffed that Phil hadn't been totally forthcoming with her. She'd once trusted him like a brother, but clearly he didn't feel the same way, if he ever had.

Finding a parking spot near the door, she opened the car windows for Bear. "Stay put. I'll only be a few minutes." She beelined to the bakery section at the back of the store, feeling guilty she hadn't thought to stock up on brownies at Death by Chocolate before it closed. The store-bought ones weren't even in the same league. Tonight, though, they would have to do. She grabbed a quart of ice cream to top them off, then headed for the cash register.

Lost in her thoughts as she walked to the express lane, she almost bumped into a man headed in the same direction with a deli salad in his hands.

"Kaylee, hi." Phil glanced at the desserts she carried and raised his eyebrows. "I thought it was my sister who was responsible for all the ice cream and brownies in your dorm room. Rough day?"

Knowing she was being silly — the man was NSA, after all, and it was his job to keep secrets — Kaylee stifled the impulse to call him out on his evasiveness. Pasting on a smile, she opted not to follow suit. She'd tell him everything she knew. *Even though he probably already knows it anyway, since he was a day ahead of me in going after the surveillance footage.*

"Not at all," she said brightly. "The children were great, as you saw. And after they left, Deputy Brooks gave us the good news they'd located Tabitha's car in the ferry parking lot." She paused and squinted up at him to give him the opportunity to admit he already had that information.

He didn't.

Her grip on the package of brownies tightened.

"Will that be all?" The cashier pointed to the carton of ice cream and brownies Kaylee hadn't yet placed on the conveyor belt.

"Oh yes, sorry." Kaylee set them down, then said to Phil, "So it looks as if Tabitha simply went off island and neglected to tell her son." For Tabitha's sake, since she clearly had nothing to do with the break-in and didn't deserve to be pestered by a couple of NSA agents, Kaylee opted not to mention Tad's text to Jessica about Tabitha visiting her sister.

Phil frowned. "The question is why?"

Oops. Her omission apparently raised more suspicions about Tabitha in his mind than it had settled. "It was her birthday yesterday. She probably just decided to get away for a little while." Kaylee ran her debit card through the reader, then collected her grocery bag. "I'm afraid I've got to run. Bear's waiting for me in the car. My ice cream is melting and I have a pizza getting cold."

Phil's eyes crinkled with amusement, his concerns about Tabitha seemingly forgotten. "Sounds like a better dinner than mine." He set his salad down on the conveyer belt for the cashier to ring through. "Enjoy. And I'll see you Monday afternoon."

Outside, Kaylee found that her dog certainly hadn't been bored while she had been shopping. Bear's nose was stuck through the cracked window, and Reese stood beside the door petting the dog's muzzle.

"Are you here for brownies and ice cream too?" Kaylee said in greeting.

Reese smiled, but his expression quickly sobered when he saw Phil stepping outside behind Kaylee. "I ran out of eggs."

Kaylee nodded, discomfited by his flat tone. "Have you eaten supper, because I'm—"

"Yeah, I have. And I need to get back to my place. I have some renovation plans to finish that I promised to deliver to a client first thing Monday morning."

"I see."

He started off, then turned back as if relenting. "Did you and Jess crack Tabitha's password and get a name for her date?"

Kaylee nodded enthusiastically. "Yep. But then Jess heard from Tad. It turns out his mom is visiting his sick aunt."

Reese shook his head, but a familiar amused twinkle returned to his eye. "I guess you're so used to stumbling on to mysteries, you've started to imagine them where they don't exist."

"To be fair, her son asked us to help him find her," Kaylee protested.

"True." Reese glanced at a vehicle pulling out of the parking lot—Phil's, if she wasn't mistaken. "I'm glad Tad's concerns turned out to be nothing. I'll see you at church tomorrow."

Kaylee sighed as she climbed into her SUV. Something was off about the way Reese had been talking to her lately. Had something she'd done given away that her feelings toward him might be growing more serious? And had that made him skittish?

She sighed again, glad she'd opted for the larger tub of ice cream.

8

Surfing the Internet for men wasn't in Kaylee's top ten preferred ways to spend a Saturday night, but since she didn't have any other plans and couldn't focus on her movie, why not try to track down the guy Tabitha was supposed to meet Thursday night?

Maybe she'd read too many of DeeDee's mystery novels, but it occurred to her that if Tabitha was being held against her will, her captor could've coerced her into feeding Tad the story about the sick aunt. And if the story was legitimate, a quick, quiet inquiry would settle their lingering concerns over how out of character it had been for Tabitha to not ensure her cat was looked after while she was gone.

Two hours later, Kaylee massaged the knot in the back of her neck. There wasn't a Ned Banford to be found in the state of Washington, and only three in the entire country—two of whom were young enough to be Tabitha's children, and the third old enough to be her grandfather.

Bear whined from his bed.

Kaylee pushed her chair back from her desk and scratched him behind the ears. "Yes, playing with you would've been a more productive use of my time." She ambled into the kitchen to make herself a cup of hot cocoa. "Either Ned Banford isn't the guy's real name, or he's a very private guy. That's not a bad thing necessarily. Except if someone's trying to contact you." Kaylee thumbed through the mail she'd tossed on the table when she got home. Looking at the return address on one of the letters, she smacked her forehead. "Why didn't I think of it sooner?"

Bear cocked his head at her tone.

"Sorry, rhetorical question." She hurried back to her computer and opened her e-mail program. Then, referencing the note she'd made earlier, she put Ned's e-mail address into the "to" line and began typing. She wrote a few sentences, then deliberated for a moment about how to close the e-mail. She didn't want it to sound as if she was suspicious of him. The e-mail alone was warning enough that if he'd taken Tabitha against her will, he hadn't gotten away unnoticed. In the end she was satisfied with the note.

> Hi Ned,
>
> I've been taking care of Tabitha's cat and was wondering if you know when she expects to return home. Her friend said she had plans to go out with you Thursday night, and since she didn't come home afterward, I'm assuming the two of you decided to keep the date going.
>
> I think her phone battery must be dead, as I haven't been able to reach her. Could you ask her to let me know how long I should continue checking in on Peony?
>
> Thanks,
>
> Kaylee Bleu

Kaylee's finger hovered over the send button. She'd refrained from including her phone number to safeguard against him tracking her down if he turned out to be a creep. But did she really want him to have her e-mail address either?

Bear's whine, this time from the depths of whatever dream his doggie brain had slipped into, sealed the answer in her mind—no.

She went to a popular e-mail provider and created a new alias, CatMinder. She copied the message from her first e-mail, then once more hovered her finger over the send button.

"Maybe I should make a quick call to Sara first," Kaylee said to Bear, even though he was sleeping. "Just to double-check that Peony wasn't missing or anything prior to Tabitha's disappearance. If Tabitha didn't know where her cat was, it could explain why she didn't make arrangements for someone to take care of Peony."

Sara's voice sounded gravelly when she answered. "Hello?"

"I'm sorry," Kaylee said. "I didn't mean to disturb you. I just wanted to ask a quick question. Did Tabitha happen to mention her cat going missing recently?"

"No," Sara answered in the same sleepy voice, so Kaylee apologized once more for disturbing her and quickly said good night.

With no further hesitation, Kaylee sent the e-mail to Ned Banford and said aloud, "Now we wait."

The next day after church, Kaylee, Reese, and the Petal Pushers and their spouses met at DeeDee's for a potluck lunch. The conversation soon turned to Tabitha, and Kaylee admitted to e-mailing Ned Banford to see what he knew about Tabitha's whereabouts. "So far I haven't heard a peep back from him," she said disappointedly.

Jessica released a frustrated sigh. "I haven't heard anything more from Tad either. I've got a really bad feeling something's not as hunky-dory as someone wants us to think it is. Oliver was totally droopy this morning. And you know that always means something's not right."

Kaylee expected to see an amused twinkle in Reese's eye at this last declaration, since he didn't put much faith in the supposed sensitivities of Jessica's lavender geranium, Oliver, no matter how many times Jessica insisted that her plant's health could predict the future.

To her surprise, Reese nodded in agreement. "I've got a weird feeling about it too," he said. "I think you were on the right track connecting her sudden disappearance to the break-in at the admiral's place."

Kaylee did a double take. Last night he'd teased her about how she made a mystery out of everything, even when there wasn't one. What had changed his mind?

"The guy's aide struck me as a little cagey," Reese went on. "And those NSA agents running security . . ." Reese glanced at Kaylee. "I know the one guy's supposed to be an old friend, but I don't trust him."

"Why not?" Kaylee asked, ignoring for the time being that she didn't trust Phil at the moment either.

Reese hesitated, as if choosing his words carefully. Finally he said slowly, "The more I think about it, the more I think the supposed break-in was a cover-up story."

"How do you mean?" DeeDee asked.

"I think the Newtons broke their own window to trigger the alarm."

Kaylee furrowed her brow. "Why would they do that?"

"Your guess is as good as mine," Reese said. "But what I do know is that whoever broke the window was already inside the house, because almost all the shattered glass was on the ground *outside*."

Kaylee stared at him, stunned that he had withheld such a potentially major clue. "Why didn't you mention that when we were there?"

Reese's expression turned contrite. "I knew something was off about the scene when I arrived, but I didn't clue in to the significance of where the glass was until a client called me last night to board up a window their kid blew out with a stray baseball."

Kaylee pulled out her cell phone. "I should tell Phil."

"I called him last night." Reese tapped his leg, appearing uneasy, as if he didn't want to hurt her by saying something against her friend, but clearly feeling that it needed to be said. "It didn't seem to be news to him."

Kaylee's chest tightened. She'd looked up to her roommate's big brother for years. His stories about foiling the bad guys had partly inspired her decision to offer her expertise as a forensic botanist to law enforcement over the years. The notion that Phil might have deliberately misled her was painful.

"Maybe we're approaching this all wrong," Mary piped up. "We've assumed Tabitha saw the prowler and was silenced because of it, but what if she *was* the prowler?"

"Tabitha?" DeeDee repeated, sounding as baffled by Mary's theory as the rest of them appeared.

"It would explain why she asked her son to call off the search," Mary added.

"I can't believe Tabitha would break into a house," Jessica said.

"Fair enough," Mary said. "I don't know the woman. But based on Reese's observation about the glass, the break-in could've been staged, right? And maybe Tabitha was at the house innocently, stopping by to introduce herself in much the same way as Kaylee when she hopped the fence to speak to Mrs. Newton."

Kaylee nodded. "If Mrs. Newton panicked at the sight of Tabitha the way she did me, only with no help at hand, I could see her triggering the house alarm to summon law enforcement."

"Or maybe Mrs. Newton jumped to other conclusions about

why a strange woman was at her home," Mary's husband, Herb, suggested. "If she lost her cool with Tabitha, it would explain why the poor woman might've raced over the fence and through her own garden."

"That could explain the frosty tension I noticed among the Newton family too," Reese added.

"Might explain the broken window as well," DeeDee's husband, Andy, contributed.

DeeDee quirked an eyebrow at him. "How do you figure?"

"Once Tabitha was gone and Mrs. Newton no longer felt threatened, she might not want to explain her initial suspicions to the deputy." Andy explained. "Better to pretend there'd been a real prowler than admit she'd overreacted to the presence of a woman who, for all she knew, could've been there to see her son or her husband's aide without her permission. I got the impression the Newtons like their privacy, yes?"

Tapping her fingers to her lips, Kaylee considered the theory. It could explain the cat fur on Diane's slacks. If Diane had overheard Kaylee say Tabitha must've seen the prowler, she might have assumed Tabitha was, in fact, the person she'd surprised and gone to confront her.

"But where is Tabitha now?" Jessica asked. "Do you think she was so mortified at being mistaken for a prowler that she went into hiding?"

Mary shrugged. "Going to take care of a sick aunt would've been the perfect excuse. And she could have been so flustered by what went down at Pennybrook Grove that she completely forgot to make arrangements for her cat."

"I'd feel a whole lot better if I could talk to Tabitha, or even Tad," Jessica said with a skeptical frown. "Nothing about this feels right to me."

During the bus ride from town Monday afternoon, Kaylee was careful to explain to the camp kids how important it was that they all remain on their best behavior, since the Newtons had given them permission to visit. However, as she, DeeDee, and Sara herded the students from Pennybrook Grove's entrance toward the island's oldest tree, a boy caught a glimpse of some kind of animal and was twenty yards in the opposite direction before Kaylee noticed.

"I'm on it," Sara said, already sprinting away.

"There's one in every group," DeeDee said to Kaylee over the heads of the remaining students.

"Okay, kids," Kaylee said, as they neared the Newtons' impressive arboretum. "Who can guess which of these trees is the island's oldest?"

A handful of children pointed to a nearby conifer standing more than two hundred feet tall.

Kaylee smiled, having anticipated the guess. "That's a good try. This isn't the oldest tree, but the *Pseudotsuga menziesii* is the third tallest tree species in the world, after the redwood and the mountain ash."

The children gave her puzzled expressions.

Kaylee smiled. "*Pseudotsuga menziesii* is the tree's scientific name. It's Latin. Who can tell me why scientists call plants by Latin names, instead of their common names?"

The hand of a pigtailed girl of about nine or ten shot into the air.

"Yes?" Kaylee pointed to the girl.

"Because people in other countries speak different languages and might have different names than we do for our pine trees," the youngster said. "But if they call it by its Latin name, all the other scientists will know which tree they're talking about."

"Very good. Here in North America, for example, we call this tree a Douglas fir." Kaylee briefly explained the difference between firs and pines, then drew the group's attention to the five-foot-wide stump of a felled *Pseudotsuga menziesii*. "Who knows how we can figure out this tree's age when it was chopped down?"

This time, a dozen hands shot into the air. While the children spent the next few minutes counting the rings on the stump, Kaylee glanced around to see what was keeping Sara and the boy she'd chased after.

Kaylee spotted the teacher slowly winding through the trees, holding the boy's hand. To her surprise, Ryan Newton kept stride beside her. Given that it had taken him less than a minute to ask Kaylee if she had dinner plans the day they met, Kaylee could imagine he was having a similar conversation with Sara. *I should've warned her about him ahead of time, not that I'd expected to see him.*

DeeDee elbowed Kaylee. "Does 190 sound right?"

Kaylee returned her attention to the group. "Absolutely." She spent a few more minutes telling them about the uses of fir lumber, with "as a Christmas tree" being voted the favorite.

The smallest girl tilted her head way back in an attempt to see the very top of the Douglas fir. "How do people fit them in their houses?"

Everyone laughed. "They use smaller ones, goofball," her brother explained.

Kaylee clapped her hands to draw everyone's attention away from the girl and couldn't help but see that she'd also managed to attract Phil's notice. He stood next to a copse of Pacific madrone and nodded hello when they made eye contact.

"Okay, boys and girls," she said, ignoring the odd tingling his gaze sent down her spine. "One more guess at which tree here is the island's oldest."

The young boy who'd run away earlier now raced over to a gnarly old Garry oak and yelled, "This one!"

The children all murmured in agreement.

"Appearances can be deceiving," Kaylee said. "Although this tree is probably much older than your grandparents."

"Not mine," a towheaded boy piped up. "My grandmother's so old she doesn't have her own teeth anymore, and I counted almost as many wrinkles on her face as that big tree stump."

A giggle burst from the shrubs to Kaylee's right and she spotted Diane pressing her fingers to her lips, her eyes dancing with amusement while Shawn stood beside her, stone-faced. Kaylee hadn't realized she'd have a wider audience than her campers. Ryan had wandered off, as had Phil, but now both the admiral's wife and his aide seemed to be listening in.

Kaylee directed the children's focus to a *Juniperus occidentalis*. "This, ladies and gentlemen, is our island's oldest tree."

The children peered up to its peak, which didn't top much more than fifty feet. Based on the tittering and giggles, it appeared they were unimpressed.

"This is a western juniper. Many of you probably have small shrubs of it planted around your home. They are extremely slow growing, which is why it's so small compared to the fir we were just looking at. But this particular tree is actually more than 600 years old."

Gasps went around the group.

The pigtailed girl asked, "How do you know? You can't count the rings inside unless you chop it down."

"That's a good question." Kaylee explained the process of taking core samples to measure a tree's age. "So this tree was here long before we were even a country. Imagine the history it's seen."

After Kaylee answered a few more questions, DeeDee took over, sharing stories through history the tree might've witnessed. The children stood spellbound.

Kaylee took the opportunity to slip away from the group and speak to Diane. "Thank you again for allowing us to bring the children here today. The estate has such an impressive array of trees. It makes teaching about them so much easier."

"I've enjoyed listening in," Diane said politely.

"I was hoping I'd get a chance to chat with you alone." Despite Diane's skeptical expression, Kaylee continued. "I still haven't gotten in touch with your neighbor." Which was technically true: Tad claimed he had heard from Tabitha, but there was only a text from his number to vouch for it.

"And?" Diane asked frostily.

"And we got to thinking—what if those footprints in her garden were hers? Could you tell if the prowler you surprised was a woman?"

Diane shook her head, but a spark in her eyes told Kaylee she wasn't being truthful.

Kaylee went on. "I know what my first thought would be if I happened upon a pretty blonde in my house with three men staying there on their own."

Diane seemed to give a little. "That she was a friend of my son's? Yes, it did occur to me. But girlfriends don't break into the house when their boyfriend isn't home."

"But the house wasn't actually broken into, was it? I mean, the window was broken later for the police's benefit, wasn't it?"

"That's absurd!"

The students went instantly silent and gaped across the yard at them.

"It was absurd," DeeDee said. She carried on her story as

if Diane's exclamation had been a commentary on it, and the children's attention returned to DeeDee.

"The glass was on the ground outside the house," Kaylee whispered. "That means the window was broken from the inside."

Diane's eyes narrowed. "This is none of your business."

"It is if you had anything to do with Tabitha's disappearance. I know you were in her house. I saw the cat hair on your slacks."

Diane's eyes widened with shock, but she quickly recovered. "Don't be ridiculous. I was visiting a friend with a cat."

Kaylee inwardly winced. She'd taken a gamble with the allegation, knowing there could be another explanation.

Shawn must have gone to fetch Admiral Newton when Kaylee and Diane's conversation became heated, because the admiral suddenly appeared striding across the yard toward them, his aide flanking him.

"Tell Mark to remove Miss Bleu from the grounds," the admiral commanded his aide, who immediately signaled Phil's NSA compatriot.

Mark made a beeline for Kaylee, his expression fierce. As he approached her, however, one of the students shrieked, "That man has a gun!"

9

DeeDee and Sara had the children hit the dirt faster than the admiral could start damage control.

Admiral Newton shot Kaylee a seething glare as he motioned for Mark to stand down, then walked over to the group of children. "It's okay, kids. This man is a security guard. He works for me. He's not going to shoot anyone. You can stand up."

DeeDee and Sara righted themselves first and then encouraged the children to do so. A couple of the kids were sniffling, and some were shaking, but a few seemed curious.

"Why does he carry a gun?" one girl asked. "Are you afraid someone's going to steal your old tree?"

Kaylee muffled a giggle.

"No, no," the admiral said. "Nothing like that. I'm sorry he frightened you."

"Can we see the gun?" a boy asked.

"You don't need to see the gun," Sara said firmly. "We're here to learn about trees."

"Indeed," the admiral said. "But it's probably best if you return to your bus now."

At a glance from DeeDee, Kaylee mouthed, "Stall."

DeeDee nodded almost imperceptibly. "Which tree is your favorite?" she asked the admiral as he attempted to steer the group toward the bus, clearly not used to subordinates who didn't obey without question.

Kaylee took advantage of DeeDee's delay tactics to raise an eyebrow at Diane. Diane clenched her jaw and glanced from Mark, who was still holding his ground about ten feet away, to her husband being inundated with questions from the children after DeeDee's example.

"All right, yes." Diane finally expelled the words like a bite of rotten fruit. "I saw a woman running toward the back door the instant I stepped into the house. The next thing I knew, the alarm was blaring. I suppose it was armed, and in my surprise at seeing someone in the house, I failed to type in the security code to disarm it. Or maybe the woman set it off when she broke the window in her panic to get out. I don't know."

Kaylee pulled out her phone and showed Diane the photograph of Tabitha that Tad had sent. "Is this the woman you saw?"

Diane shrugged. "I didn't see her clearly," she said as Phil and Ryan approached them. "She was a blonde, but if she really expected me to think she was the new housekeeper, she wouldn't have run."

Phil snapped to attention at her mention of a housekeeper. "You never told us you spoke to the prowler."

"Tabitha is a housekeeper. Did you hire her?" Kaylee asked the admiral's aide, but Shawn shook his head in response.

"I never spoke to her," Diane said to Phil. She reached into her pocket and produced a business card with perforated edges that looked as though it had been made on a home computer. "But she dropped this on her way out. Calico Cleaning? The card's bogus." Diane slanted a glance at her son. "I tried the number. It's for a sushi place."

Kaylee reached for the card, but Phil took it by the edges, presumably before she could contaminate it with more fingerprints.

"I yelled out the door after the woman," Diane went on. "But I couldn't see which way she went. Part of me was glad she was gone. My husband certainly doesn't need the bad optics of a strange woman discovered in his house. He's seen too many high-ranking officials' careers sabotaged that way." Her glance sliced from the admiral's aide to her son. "Unfortunately, it's been more difficult to inspire the same caution in the younger generation."

"Mother, I already told you," Ryan protested. "I would never leave a girl alone at the house."

Diane grabbed the phone out of Kaylee's hand and shoved it toward Ryan's face. "You're telling me you don't know this woman?"

Ryan glanced at the photo, then his gaze went past the children now being escorted to the bus to Tabitha's property. "This is our neighbor?"

"Yes," Kaylee said.

"But you don't know if she's the woman you saw?" he asked his mom.

"Do you know her?" Phil reiterated.

Ryan shrugged. "She looks familiar. I've likely seen her around. But no, I don't *know* her. And I certainly didn't let her into the house."

The admiral pried himself away from the departing students and strode their way, leaving Mark to watch over the bus boarding.

Knowing she was seconds away from being booted off the property, Kaylee blurted, "So how did she get in without setting off the alarm?"

All eyes turned to Shawn.

"I don't know," he said defensively. "There was no one here when the three of us left for dinner at five, and the admiral and Ryan both saw me arm the security system before we left."

"That's true," Ryan agreed.

The admiral stormed up to their small group, but before he could get a single angry word out, Sara came scurrying up behind him, clasping a youngster's hand. "Excuse me. We're a little desperate here. Could we use your washroom before we go?"

The admiral flicked his fingers toward his aide. "Escort them inside, will you?"

Shawn cupped Sara's elbow and steered her toward the back door, looking relieved at the excuse to extract himself from the break-in discussion.

"As I said before," the admiral hissed to Kaylee, "this is none of your business. Phil, please see her to the bus. Now."

Kaylee may have asked Diane everything she'd intended, but she had lots of questions for Phil too. Now probably wasn't the best time, but they had to wait for Sara to return anyway. She took a deep breath and jumped right in. "Diane said the intruder broke the window on her way out. So was there any evidence she'd broken into the house in the first place?"

"I can't discuss this with you."

"Clearly the admiral is worried about a breach of national security if he summoned NSA agents to his vacation home. Or was he worried about a personal secret getting out?"

"The admiral is as moral as they come," Phil said, his tone clipped, sounding nothing like his usual self.

"Except that he lied to Deputy Brooks by blaming mischievous kids for the break-in."

Phil eyeballed the children watching them from the bus windows. "It was the simplest way to let the matter go."

"Because whoever was inside the house didn't break in. Someone must've given her a key and the security code. Was it Ryan? Or Shawn?"

Phil motioned to the bus door. "You need to leave."

Kaylee started to go, then opted to try a different tack. "Were you summoned to take care of her?" she asked softly, not entirely sure what she meant by "take care of." Surely the man she'd always considered a friend wouldn't be involved in silencing a witness?

"Kaylee, I haven't 'taken care of' your missing friend," Phil said, his voice measured. "In fact, I'm as eager to find her and get some straight answers as you are. You need to trust me."

Kaylee gazed back at him for a long moment, wondering whether or not to tell him what Tad had texted about Tabitha being at his aunt's. Ultimately, she stopped herself. She wasn't entirely sure if trusting Phil was a smart move.

Once camp was finished for the day, Kaylee and DeeDee met up with Jessica and Mary at Death by Chocolate.

Jessica's usually neatly coiffed hair appeared as if she'd been raking her fingers through it. "I don't know what to think," she said as the women settled at a table. "I've tried more than half a dozen times to call and text Tad, but he's not answering. It isn't like him."

"Well, I managed to extract new information from the Newtons," Kaylee said. "Mrs. Newton wasn't expected home and arrived to find a blonde woman in the house. If Mrs. Newton can be believed, the woman broke the window in her panic to get out." Kaylee filled in the rest of the details.

"If the woman was in the house, someone must've given her a key and the security code," Mary said.

Kaylee nodded. "It would seem so. But if she was a girlfriend, why didn't she simply say so? And why did the admiral summon NSA agents in on the red-eye after the incident?"

"Maybe neither his aide nor his son was man enough to fess up to *gross misconduct*," DeeDee theorized.

"I wondered that myself," Kaylee said, "but I think if that's all that was going on here, Phil would've told me. I'm betting whoever was in the house must have gotten away with something important."

"Important how?" Mary asked.

Kaylee shrugged. "I don't know what kind of sensitive information an admiral would have, but he's heading to Hawaii to lead the navy's entire fleet down there. He could have battle plans, deployment plans, installation plans. Who knows what? But I suspect it's information the enemy would pay a high price for."

DeeDee shuddered. "I'm starting to feel as if we're in the middle of a James Bond movie."

"Well, there's no way you can convince me Tabitha was the blonde who stole that stuff," Jessica said. "More likely, someone wore a wig and set her up to take the fall. Maybe conveniently helped her vanish to make her look guiltier." Jessica stared hard at her coffee cup, shaking her head. "I can't believe the sheriff's department isn't taking her disappearance more seriously."

"Kaylee, have you heard anything back from the guy Tabitha was supposed to meet Thursday night?" Mary asked.

Kaylee quickly checked her dummy e-mail on her phone. "No, he still hasn't responded." She caught sight of the time. "I probably should go check on the cat now. Bear wasn't happy about my leaving him at home this afternoon, even though I knew he wouldn't be welcome at Pennybrook Grove. I promised him I wouldn't be late."

As Kaylee rose to leave, DeeDee grabbed her arm and pointed out the front window. "Wait a second. Isn't that Ryan Newton?"

Jessica and Mary twisted in their seats to follow DeeDee's finger.

Ryan stood on the other side of the street, casually leaning against a light post and chatting with an attractive woman.

"I thought he was interested in you, Kaylee," Jessica commented.

"From what I've seen," Kaylee said, "he tries his luck with every woman who crosses his path."

"But that's not just any woman," Mary said. "She's Sammy's daughter."

"Did you see that?" DeeDee exclaimed. "He slipped her an envelope."

Kaylee frowned in confusion. "Who's Sammy and what's the big deal about Ryan slipping her an envelope?"

"Sammy was a bookie who'd give anyone odds on just about any game or race going," Mary explained. "He went down about a year before you took over the flower shop. But rumor has it that his daughter took over the family business."

Kaylee frowned at Ryan and the woman, still chatting amicably. "That's interesting. Phil mentioned Ryan is between jobs. And I saw him hit his mom up for some cash the other day."

Mary tapped her chin. "Well, if he's lost a few bets, it'd give him motive to rob from his own house, using a girlfriend as an accomplice to make it look like a random burglary."

"Tabitha wouldn't do that," Jessica insisted.

"Then maybe she saw the woman who did," DeeDee said. "If Ryan's girlfriend was worried about being identified by Tabitha, it would've given him motive to make sure she didn't talk."

Kaylee cringed at Jessica's sickly pallor. Ryan did seem like the impetuous type. But was he capable of killing someone?

"Who's that?" Mary asked, pointing out the window, where the admiral's aide had supplanted Sammy's daughter and seemed to be holding a heated discussion with Ryan.

"His name is Shawn, and he works for the admiral," Kaylee said. And if he knew Ryan was dancing on the wrong side of the law, Phil must too. If the irresponsible behavior of a shiftless son threatened to embarrass the family, it would explain the chilly tension in the Newton household.

"I don't like this," Jessica said.

"Me neither," Kaylee replied. Was Tabitha the prowler? Did she go into hiding because Mrs. Newton spotted her? Or did she disappear because she too saw the prowler? And if that was the case, did she disappear of her own volition?

"You hear about rich people killing off witnesses all the time," Jessica went on.

"We don't know that Tabitha is dead," Kaylee said firmly. "For all we know, she really is visiting Tad's sick aunt like he texted. Because if she isn't, why would Tad lie?"

Mila, who was helping her mother out at the bakery during her visit, paused in the process of wiping down the next table. "Are you talking about Tad Mason again?"

"Yes," Jessica said hesitantly, appearing slightly sheepish. Apparently she hadn't told her daughter about the favor Tad had requested.

"He doesn't have an aunt," Mila said.

"Are you sure?" Kaylee asked.

"Positive. When we were dating, he was always envying the family get-togethers we had with all my cousins. He told me his dad was an only child. His mom's brother never married and died before he was born."

Jessica slowly nodded as if latent memories had begun to trickle back into her mind. "I knew the story didn't feel right."

"Do you think Tad would've assumed you'd share his text with Mila?" Kaylee asked.

Jessica's brow furrowed. "I don't know. Maybe."

"If he's still as sweet on her as he was back in high school, I'm sure he hoped." Mary winked at Mila, who blushed a deep red.

"So it's possible," Kaylee theorized, "that he hoped Mila

would remember he had no aunts and that he chose to send a text claiming his mom was visiting one as a clue."

"So we'd realize he'd been coerced into calling off the search for his mother," Jessica declared, sounding as if everything finally made sense again.

Kaylee occasionally wondered whether Jessica's love of conspiracy theories got a little out of hand, but this time she had to consider the fact that her friend just might be right.

10

Kaylee rose early Tuesday morning to feed Peony and run an errand for that day's camp activity before opening The Flower Patch. The sun shone bright in a perfect blue sky, its rays causing the dewy grass around Wildflower Cottage to sparkle. It was as if all of nature were celebrating the dawn of a new spring. Soon the fields outside her cottage would be filled with the sweet scent of lavender.

Such a beautiful day would have made it easy for Kaylee to push aside her fretful theories of what could've become of Tabitha . . . if not for Mila's revelation.

Did Tad *really* want them to give up the search for his mom? Or had he been coerced?

Since he hadn't answered any of Jessica's calls or texts, Kaylee suspected the latter. Unfortunately, she wouldn't have time to search for more clues at Tabitha's when she stopped by to feed the cat—she had nettles to collect for the spring break camp.

I can't wait to see the children's faces when I tell them they'll be cooking with weeds that sting your legs when you brush against them. Kaylee loaded the box of supplies she'd gathered for the afternoon workshop into her car, then glanced around for Bear. "C'mon boy," she called out, scanning the yard. "We've got lots of work to do this morning."

Bear raced from behind the house as quickly as his little dachshund legs could carry him and leaped into the car.

Kaylee laughed. "I guess you didn't want to be left home again, huh?"

She drove to Tabitha's house and peered through the trees

toward the Newton estate as she unlocked the back door. The grounds were quiet, not that she expected to see anything, except maybe Mark or Phil patrolling the perimeter. The calico burst out the door the instant Kaylee opened it, so she fetched the food and water dish and set them out on the back stoop. The cat was so eager to explore, she didn't even twine around Kaylee's legs in her usual purring way. And she totally ignored Bear barking excitedly in the car at the sight of her hopping onto the top rail of the fence.

"Enjoy the day, Peony," Kaylee said. "I'll be back tonight to let you inside." She walked over to the cat and scratched her behind her ears. "Maybe you can dig up some clues as to the whereabouts of your mistress while I'm gone, hmm?"

Peony stretched her hind leg and proceeded to groom herself, as if Tabitha's whereabouts were the least of her concerns.

Kaylee sighed as she returned to her SUV. If both the woman's son and her own cat weren't concerned about her disappearance, why did it prey so heavily on Kaylee's mind?

She shooed Bear from the driver's seat and climbed in, then backed out of the driveway. "I know you want to make friends with her, but we have lots to do. You'll get to come out at the next stop, okay?"

Bear flopped down on the seat, looking forlorn.

Kaylee consulted the address Reese had given her for the sheep farm where he'd been repairing doors and drove the few miles farther out of town. When she'd mentioned needing to pick nettles for a camp activity, he'd told her he'd seen a meadow filled with nettles next to the sheep pasture. She glanced at her dashboard clock and hoped he was right.

She spotted his pickup before the farm's house number. The truck sat in the lane leading to the barn, so she parked behind it, grabbed her basket and Bear's leash, and climbed out. "No chasing cats, lambs, or any other creature you see," Kaylee cautioned her little dog.

He leaned against her leg at the woeful bleating coming from the sheep pen, not appearing the least bit interested in venturing beyond the reach of his leash.

Reese waved from the doorway of the barn. "You made it. I'll show you where you can find your nettles, but first you've got to come see this." He led her down the center path of the old hipped-roof barn and out the back door into another sheep pen. Inside, a newborn lamb was making his first attempts to wobble to his feet as his mother licked him clean.

Kaylee's heart melted at the sight, and even Bear seemed transfixed. "How adorable."

Reese grinned. "I work at a lot of farms, and I never get tired of seeing something like that."

"I love spring," Kaylee said. "The smell of the earth after a gentle rain, the sound of birds singing again, the sight of plants reawakening, and the joy of new life like this."

"Definitely a much-needed boost after a long hard winter."

"Remember this week's sermon at church? It's God's way of reminding us that just as good comes from the dormancy of winter, it can come from dark times in our lives too."

Reese nodded. "Like bringing you here after you lost your professor job."

"Yes." Kaylee drew in a deep breath, inhaling the sweet and not-so-sweet scents of the farm and surrounding countryside. "And now with Tabitha missing, I think I needed the reminder there are still many good and beautiful things in this world."

Reese slung an arm around her shoulder. He seemed as if he wanted to say something, but he didn't, so they just stood there for a long, comfortably quiet moment, smiling at the fuzzy lamb testing its wobbly legs in the lush green grass.

"Did you hear two new baby orcas have been spotted offshore?" Reese asked at last.

"Are you serious?" Kaylee's heart leaped. Watching for whales had always been one of her favorite pastimes when she'd visited her grandparents here as a youngster—a passion she hadn't outgrown.

"Maybe we could go for a walk along the shore sometime, try to catch sight of them?" Reese suggested.

"I'd love that. With any luck, it will help me relax." Kaylee rubbed her temples. "This sketchy situation with what went down at the Newtons' has me really unsettled. Jess has conjured up all these conspiracy theories that are starting to sound a little too plausible."

Reese faced her with a frown. "I have to admit that you going out to Tabitha's place alone every day to check on the cat worries me. If the Newtons were concerned about what Tabitha might've seen, they can't be too thrilled about you and your friends asking questions."

Kaylee caught herself squirming at the memory of the admiral's reaction to her conversation with Diane yesterday.

"And I know that NSA agent is the brother of an old friend, but I'm not sure he can be trusted," Reese said, echoing her own thoughts over the past few days. Kaylee began to protest, but Reese cut her off. "I'm not saying he's not a nice guy. But he's a government agent, and his first loyalty has to be to the job, to national security."

"Sure. But he wouldn't throw me under the bus for the greater good."

Reese's expression told her he wasn't so sure. He squeezed her hand. "Promise me you'll be careful."

"I promise."

He searched her gaze. "You know I really care about you, right?"

Her heart somersaulted at the honesty gleaming in his eyes. "Yes."

"Overhearing you and Phil reminisce about your college days . . ." Reese's voice trailed off.

My college days? Was Reese referring to Kaylee laughing over the old river mishap at camp registration? He must be. She couldn't recall doing much other reminiscing with Phil.

"It made me realize," Reese went on, "there is so much about you, about your past, about the things that have shaped you, that I don't know. And I want to."

Heat climbed into Kaylee's cheeks. "I feel that way too."

"How about I go with you tonight when you check in on Tabitha's cat, and then we can go out for dinner afterward?"

Kaylee's heart swelled at the invitation, and for a moment, she couldn't quite catch her breath. "I'd like that," she finally managed.

"Great. I'll pick you up around six?"

"Perfect." Kaylee glanced at her watch and groaned. "I'd better start collecting the nettles I need or I'll be late opening the flower shop."

Reese walked her and Bear to the gate and pointed out a field where she'd find a good supply.

Kaylee pulled on the gardening gloves she'd brought along for the job and gave Bear's leash a tug. He planted his rear end in the dirt and braced his front legs.

"What's wrong?" Kaylee asked her dog.

Bear eyed the field warily.

"You've got fur," she said. "The nettles won't sting you. Just don't stick your nose in them."

Bear didn't look convinced, and Reese broke into laughter.

"You're not helping," she scolded.

"You're right. If you'd like me to try being helpful, I can

watch him while you collect your nettles."

"Thanks. I appreciate it." She smiled at Reese and handed over Bear's leash.

Twenty minutes later, she had a basketful of prickly nettles on her car's back seat and was headed for town. She had rolled down the window, and Bear savored the warm spring air tousling his ears.

Kaylee squinted through the windshield at an approaching dark pickup. "That looks like Phil," she said to Bear, who wasn't paying the least bit of attention. She waved as they passed, but apparently he didn't see her. She watched his vehicle in her rearview mirror, and when it turned onto the little-used rural road she'd just passed, she slowed and pulled onto the shoulder. "What's he doing heading out into the middle of nowhere? There's nothing but fields and an old abandoned cabin down that road."

Bear whined, apparently missing the wind in his face.

Suspicious, Kaylee signaled her intention to do a U-turn and Bear's whine grew louder. "I want to see what he's up to," Kaylee said defensively. "We won't be long."

As she headed back in the direction she'd come, Phil's truck reappeared on the main road ahead. Had he made a wrong turn? She glanced at the dashboard clock. She could afford to take a few minutes to see where he went. On the third left turn, which had them going back in the direction she'd been going in the first place, she started to have serious doubts that he knew where he was going. But a few minutes later, he parked outside Filibuster, an upscale steakhouse.

Kaylee parked a few rows away, debating whether to hang around to see if Phil was meeting someone or if he had just decided to go out for breakfast. She watched him through the restaurant window chatting with the hostess.

Bear pawed at her arm.

"Okay, yes, we'll go." Filibuster wasn't the kind of place Kaylee could go in and pretend she'd stopped by for a quick to-go order.

As she twisted in her seat to back out of her parking place, Phil reemerged from the restaurant. She wouldn't follow him again. She was supposed to open The Flower Patch in twenty minutes, and Mary wasn't coming in until noon.

But Kaylee couldn't help herself.

Phil turned right out of the parking lot—not the way he'd go if he were heading back to the Newton estate—so Kaylee turned right too. A quarter mile outside of town, Phil swerved onto a side road.

Kaylee slowed. A stone-gray cloud she hadn't noticed before chose that moment to blot out the sun. Kaylee stopped at the intersection, her heart racing. Should she follow Phil? Dense stands of trees lined both sides of this little-used gravel road, making it appear even darker.

She waited until his truck passed a bend in the road, then, taking a deep breath, turned onto it. She drove cautiously, being sure to stay far enough back so he wouldn't see her through the trees. Of course, that also meant she couldn't see him.

For another quarter mile, the dust churned up on the road ahead of her was the only sign she was still on his tail.

Crawling around the next bend, she jolted.

Phil's truck was driving down the middle of the road—toward her.

She edged toward the ditch alongside the road to give him room to pass. "Please don't recognize me. Please don't recognize me," she whispered.

He veered straight for her.

Her heart jumped into her throat. She slammed on the brakes.

The oncoming pickup screeched to a stop mere feet in front of hers, dust billowing around it. Phil jumped out, a gun in his hand.

A gun? Kaylee's breath froze in her lungs.

He sighted her down the gun's barrel and bellowed, "Get out of the car!"

Her hands shot into the air. "Phil, it's me, Kaylee," she called through her open window.

Every inch of her body trembled. Why did she have to follow Phil? She'd promised Reese she'd be careful.

She lifted her gaze to meet Phil's and his icy glare sent a shiver down her spine.

Bear yipped frantically as Phil drew closer, his gun still trained on her windshield.

"I know who you are," he said, his tone harsher than she'd ever heard, not sounding like the Phil she knew at all.

Reese's words—*I'm not sure he can be trusted*—slammed through her mind.

Had she ever really known this man? Paralyzed with fear, Kaylee could only stare at the muzzle of Phil's gun.

He stopped a few feet from her door. "Now get out of the car."

11

Ice in her veins, Kaylee peeked at the rearview mirror. Could she back down the winding road fast enough to hit the main highway before Phil got back to his truck? Not if he blew out her tire. Or worse.

But did a smart person really climb out of her car in the middle of the woods when a madman was pointing a weapon at her?

Phil must've guessed what she was thinking because he shoved his gun into some hidden holster and held up his hands to show he wasn't a threat. "C'mon, Kaylee, get out of the car. We need to talk."

She felt marginally relieved with the gun out of sight, but she remained in her car. "I can hear you fine from here. Go ahead and talk."

Amusement twinkled in his eyes. "You've got spunk. I'll give you that. I'm sorry I pulled the gun on you, but I was trying to make a point. What were you thinking following a strange vehicle down a deserted road?"

"I was thinking I was following my old friend Phil Haynes, a respectable government agent. Someone I could *trust*." She spit out the last word with enough disdain to make it clear that she no longer felt that way.

Phil's expression took on a pained edge. "You can trust me, Kaylee. But you need to understand that sometimes—a lot of times—it's difficult to tell your enemies from your friends."

She squinted at him. "What are you saying? You can't possibly think I'm an enemy."

"I'm saying that, for your own safety, you need to stop this little sleuthing game you're playing."

"Little sleuthing game?" she repeated indignantly. "A woman is missing. Trust me, this is *not* a game to me."

"Still—"

"Was Tabitha the woman Mrs. Newton found in the house?" Kaylee demanded, regaining her confidence Phil wasn't a threat to her.

"I can't discuss the case with you, Kaylee."

"So that's a yes."

Phil huffed in frustration, which she took as further confirmation. Bear whined, clearly wishing she'd leave the guy in her dust. Kaylee tugged the little dog into her arms and reassured him with a gentle hug as she pressed Phil for more answers.

"Do you know where Tabitha is now?" she asked.

"No."

Kaylee studied him, trying to decide if his response had come out a little too quickly and adamantly to be believed. What she did know was that they couldn't have a productive discussion while she remained in her car. She set Bear back on the passenger seat and told him to stay, then climbed out. As she stood facing Phil, Reese's warning about him echoed through her thoughts once more.

She squared her shoulders and gazed unflinchingly into Phil's eyes. "Who let Tabitha in the house? Was it Ryan? Shawn? Mrs. Newton clearly figured she needed to whitewash someone's dirty laundry for the sake of the police report."

Phil's rigid stance loosened. He lifted a boot onto her car's bumper and casually rested his forearm on his thigh as if he were sincerely attempting to appear casual. "Mrs. Newton jumped to erroneous conclusions."

"How can you be so sure?"

"You're not the only one investigating, and I think I've made more progress than you."

Kaylee crossed her arms over her chest, as much to ward off the sting of his response as to give the impression she wasn't going to go away without answers. "When I saw you the other day, I imagined catching up with you being a whole lot more pleasant."

Glancing away, Phil raked his fingers through his hair. "I'm sorry. The last thing I want to do is play the heavy with you." He suddenly dropped his foot back to the ground and clasped her upper arms. "But you're playing with fire. And my sister would kill me if I let you get burned."

Inside the car, Bear scratched at the side window, barking furiously.

Kaylee shook off his hands. "Is that why you told Tad to get us to stop searching for his mother? And why he hasn't answered any of Jessica's calls since?"

Surprise flared in Phil's eyes. "Did he say he knows where his mother is?"

Backing up until she bumped against the car door, Kaylee pressed her lips together.

"You need to tell me what he said," Phil insisted.

An uncomfortable feeling swamped Kaylee once more, but she answered his question. "Tad said she went to visit a sick aunt, but it was a lie. He doesn't have any aunts. That's why I figured you or one of your men coerced him into saying it, so we'd stop interfering in whatever cover-up you're orchestrating."

"I'm not 'orchestrating' anything," Phil snapped, then tempered his voice. "But I can't say the same for the men I work with or the men I work for—which is why you need to leave this investigation to me, before you go down a path I can't rescue you from."

Kaylee's head spun at the implications of what she thought he was saying. "Do you think one of your men is a double agent?"

"People do all kinds of things for all kinds of reasons. Including seemingly mild-mannered, middle-aged mothers who work as housekeepers."

Kaylee gasped. "You're talking about Tabitha? You think Tabitha Mason is—what? A spy?" The idea was so ludicrous, Kaylee laughed out loud.

"Her fingerprints were on the business card the intruder dropped. How else would you explain her presence in the house?"

Kaylee wondered briefly how Phil had matched Tabitha's fingerprints. Were they on file for some reason? Or did he lift prints from her house for comparison? She shook her head realizing it didn't really matter. What mattered was proving he was wrong about Tabitha being a spy. "Maybe she was dating Shawn or, more likely, Ryan."

"Both of them are at least ten years younger than Tabitha," Phil said, then shrugged. "Though I'm not ruling out the possibility one of them romanced her into doing the job, giving himself a perfect alibi. But I think the truth might be darker than that. And you should be glad Tabitha's son broke contact."

Utterly flabbergasted by what Phil was saying, Kaylee shook her head. "You can't honestly believe Tabitha is a spy."

Phil glanced at his watch. "Don't you have someplace to be?"

She gritted her teeth at the reminder that she was late opening the flower shop, but she wasn't leaving until she had answers. "Nothing you've said has convinced me to give up the search. If anything, it has convinced me Tabitha's probably in hiding and feeling desperately alone and vulnerable."

Phil reached into his pocket and produced a black-and-white photograph of a man in what appeared to be a Russian military uniform. "Do you recognize him?"

The image was a reproduction of an old, faded original. The man in it looked a little like the picture Kaylee had seen of

Tabitha's son, but she shook her head.

"His name is Gustav Petrov," Phil said. "He's Tabitha's brother and a Russian spy."

"But it said in the family Bible that Tabitha's maiden name is Stone, not Petrov."

"Names are easy enough to change." Phil scrubbed his hand over his bristled chin, as if debating the wisdom of saying more. Seeming to come to a decision, he continued, "We believe Tabitha either came to the U.S. to continue her brother's work or was recently recruited by him. He disappeared two years ago, and intel suggests he snuck into the States."

"That's crazy." Kaylee stared at the photo. She'd heard stories of sleeper agents, but this was Orcas Island, population less than 5,000. No military installation. No top secret government lab. No reason a spy would "sleep" here waiting to be activated. The fact that Tabitha's son was interning with a government agency in DC itched at the back of Kaylee's mind, but she shut it down. "It doesn't fit. If she's a spy, why would she up and leave?"

"She was seen."

"Okay, but leaving only draws unwanted attention. And why abandon her son without any word?" Kaylee's mind raced. "How did you know to collect surveillance tapes from every camera around the ferry parking lot before the sheriff's department even located her car?"

Phil jolted at the question. "What are you talking about? I haven't seen any surveillance tapes."

Kaylee felt the blood drain from her face. "Then was it one of those government men you're not sure you can trust? The manager of a nearby drugstore said investigators commandeered all the surveillance tapes first thing Friday morning. And it wasn't anyone from the sheriff's department. I checked."

A muscle in Phil's jaw twitched. "Maybe. Or . . ." His brow

creased, as if whatever second possibility he'd thought of was even more disconcerting. "If Tabitha failed to deliver the goods, it could've been her handler."

Kaylee resisted the impulse to ask what "the goods" were since she was pretty sure Phil wouldn't tell her anyway. She suspected he'd already divulged far more than he'd intended. Kaylee pictured Tabitha's home in her mind's eye—its lack of warmth, its feeling of being staged. Could Phil be right about her?

Could Tabitha be a spy?

And if so, had she told her son? Was that why he called off the search and stopped answering Jessica's calls? *But someone as smart as Tad wouldn't make the mistake of lying about an aunt who didn't exist to someone who would know it.*

Then again, stress caused people to make mistakes, and it often led to criminals being apprehended by law enforcement.

Kaylee gripped her door handle and stared at Bear through the car window. *What am I going to tell Jess?*

She returned her attention to Phil. "You're telling me the truth about Tabitha's son? No one from the NSA has questioned him?"

"When did he tell you his mother was visiting his aunt?"

"Saturday night."

Phil shifted his jaw from side to side pensively. "If anyone did question him, it was only to ask if he knew where she was. We didn't make the spy connection until Sunday." He crossed his arms. "At least I didn't. If we have a mole, they would've known."

"So we really don't know if Tad was coerced by the feds to call us off the scent or if he did it of his own volition to protect his mother."

"And himself," Phil added. "He's an intern in a government agency. I imagine that he'll soon be asked to leave due to his family connections, if he hasn't already. If they'd done an adequate background check, they never would've allowed him to work there in the first place, given his uncle is a known Russian spy."

Kaylee shook her head. "Even if he's never met his uncle?"

"We don't take chances with national security. His kind of position is exactly where the Russians would love to have an informant on their payroll."

Kaylee shook her head. Jessica wasn't going to take this news well. "My friend is really worried about Tad. Could you at least make sure he's okay?"

Phil strode back to his truck and opened the driver's door. He paused and fixed his gaze on Kaylee for a moment before finally answering. "I'll see what I can find out. In the meantime, you need to stay out of trouble. Okay?"

She yanked open her own car door. "Believe me. Trouble is the last thing I want."

But for whatever reason, it always seems to want me.

12

Tuesday afternoon, Kaylee set the basket of *Urtica dioica* she'd gathered on the center of the kitchen counter in the lighthouse keeper's quarters and invited the children to gather around.

While Jessica herded the stragglers, Kaylee watched her friend and wondered how she'd break Phil's bombshell to her. Since Kaylee had been late getting to The Flower Patch to open the shop and hadn't had Mary there to relieve her, she'd never gotten the chance to speak to Jessica. In fact, a steady stream of customers all morning had kept her from even having time to think about how she'd share the news.

An eager student reached out and touched one of the sprigs lying so innocently in the basket. "Ouch!" She jerked back her hand. "It stung me."

Kaylee smiled. "That's why most people call *Urtica dioica* stinging nettle."

A dark-haired girl made a disgusted face. "I'm not gonna eat that."

"Me neither," chimed in several others.

"Don't worry. Once we cook the leaves, they lose their sting," Kaylee assured them. "And you can have the fun of going home and telling your parents or older brothers and sisters you ate *stinging* nettle!"

One of the boys snatched up a sprig of nettle by its stalk and chased the girls around the room with it.

"Alex," Sara scolded. "Stop teasing the girls and put that back in the bowl."

The sprig drooped as Alex returned to the counter and he

released it with an "ow."

The girls giggled and one said, "Serves you right."

"Okay class." Kaylee donned her gloves and waited for the group to settle down. "I'm going to toss these in the pot of water we have boiling on the stove, and that will take away the sting. There are many different ways you can eat nettles. You can steep it for tea, add it to soup or sauces, or sauté it. But today, I thought we'd use it in a pasta dish. Does everyone like pasta?"

Shouts of agreement issued from the group.

"I can only eat gluten-free pasta," a little boy said.

Kaylee gestured toward the packages of spiral noodles she'd bought for the workshop, which were on the counter. "Not a problem. I bought gluten-free noodles as well as regular ones. And, to be extra safe, your mom loaned me her special pot she never uses for anything containing gluten." Kaylee indicated a second pot of water heating on the stove, and the boy nodded approval. "You can find nettles in a lot of grocery stores, or you can gather your own as I did this morning. But if you do, you'll need to wear long sleeves, pants, and gloves, and you'll want to use clippers."

"I think I'd rather eat lettuce," one of the oldest girls said.

"Lettuce is good for you," Kaylee said. "Some varieties more than others. But nettles are packed with a whopping amount of iron, calcium, vitamin K, and lots of other good stuff. Eating nettles can even combat the symptoms of hay fever and other seasonal allergies."

"Really?" Jessica asked.

"That's what people claim." Kaylee didn't have allergies herself, so she didn't actually know from personal experience. "You're supposed to start drinking a couple of cups of nettle tea a day before allergy season starts. If you suffer from allergies, you should try it."

Jessica scrutinized the leaves Kaylee pulled from the pot of boiling water with a slotted spoon. "Maybe I will."

"I probably left the leaves in the water a little too long," Kaylee said to the class as she placed the last spoonful in her colander. "You only need to leave them in until they wilt, which takes about twenty or thirty seconds." She moved the strainer she'd collected them in to the sink. "Then we run cold water over them. Now who would like to volunteer to strip the leaves from the big stems?"

Every child pressed their lips together and held their hands close to their bodies, clearly not wanting to be mistaken for volunteering.

"I promise you they won't sting." Kaylee picked up a large stem and stripped the leaves into a bowl to prove it.

One brave boy raised his hand. "I can do it."

Kaylee squirted a dollop of soap into his hands first so he could wash them, then while he took care of the nettles, she added pasta to the pots of boiling water. "Once the pasta is ready, we'll toss it with a splash of olive oil and the chopped nettles. At home, I'd also fry up some chopped garlic, but I wasn't sure if all of you would like it. Then you can season it how you like. I love mine with toasted almonds and feta cheese. Sound yummy?"

From the nose-wrinkling she saw, they weren't convinced.

Kaylee laughed. "All I ask is that you try it."

Jessica, who'd momentarily slipped outside, returned just then with a tray of chocolates. "And I brought chocolate-covered grasshoppers for dessert."

A mix of "Cool!" and "Ewww!" reactions emanated from the students, and Sara and Kaylee laughed.

"These are considered a delicacy in many parts of the world," Jessica said.

One little girl looked as if she might be sick at the mere thought of eating them.

Jessica's eyes twinkled with amusement. "I brought a few plain chocolates too for those who aren't *brave* enough to try the others."

Kaylee hid her smile at the obvious dare.

As the children helped themselves to the nettle pasta and chocolate, Jessica pulled Kaylee aside. "When I went out to get the tray, I noticed the admiral's son walking along the path to the lighthouse. Or at least pretending to."

Kaylee's brow furrowed. "What do you mean?"

Sara glanced at them curiously but stayed close by the children, supervising their serving sizes. Kaylee sent her a grateful smile.

"When I first went outside," Jessica went on, "he was looking into our cars in the parking lot. Then after he reached the path to the lighthouse, he kept glancing back at me and seemed to try to peer through the cottage windows too."

The smile Kaylee had given Sara turned into a grimace. "That's creepy."

"Yeah, especially if he didn't like you grilling his mom yesterday," Jessica said. "I asked Sara, by the way, and she confirmed Tabitha has no living relatives she knows about. Although I was thinking about it, and when Mila was little, we sometimes had her call our adult friends Aunt or Uncle rather than Mr. or Mrs. So-and-So."

"So you're changing your mind?" A wisp of hope skittered through Kaylee's chest. "Do you think maybe Tabitha did go to see Aunt So-and-So?"

Jessica sighed and shrugged. "I don't know."

"Well, I actually had an enlightening conversation with Phil before coming here, but I'll fill you in after the kids leave." Kaylee peeked out the nearest window, but saw no sign of Ryan still hanging around.

Despite their initial balking, all the children had seemed to enjoy the unusual foods, or at least they relished the idea of telling their friends and family they'd enjoyed them. Once the children finished sampling their nettle pasta and chocolate-covered insects, Kaylee asked them to help clear the tables. While Kaylee washed the dishes, Jessica and Sara led the group in a few energy-burning games in the yard outside.

Bear whined at the door.

"You like hanging out with the children more than me?" Kaylee asked with mock offense.

Bear scampered to the window bench and struggled to get his short little body up onto it. Kaylee gave him a boost so he could at least watch the children play. She glimpsed a flash of blue in the trees at the edge of the yard and her pulse jumped. She scanned the trees and spotted a man half-concealed by the bare branches. Was that Ryan? Kaylee snapped on Bear's leash and headed for the door.

The instant Kaylee rounded the building, Sara tracked Kaylee's gaze and must've spotted him too. Being closer to the stranger, Sara got there first.

Ryan stepped from the cover of the trees at whatever Sara said to him—and whatever he said to her clearly struck her as laughable. Was he trying to hit her up for a date? He seemed to do it with every woman he encountered.

By the time Kaylee had crossed the yard to join them, Ryan had left. "What did he say?" Kaylee asked Sara.

"He said he was exploring, then he asked me out to dinner." Sara rolled her eyes. "You wouldn't think someone that good-looking would be so desperate."

"I hope you said no."

Sara wiggled her eyebrows. "Now why would I turn down a free meal with a handsome guy and the perfect opportunity to question him about their prowler and Tabitha?"

"Because he could be dangerous."

"I doubt it. But to be safe, I told him I'd meet him at The Sunfish Café rather than let him pick me up."

Kaylee gnawed on her lower lip. "I still don't like it."

As Sara resumed leading the children's game, Jessica joined Kaylee and asked, "What was that all about?"

"Ryan claimed he was exploring and asked Sara out to dinner," Kaylee answered.

"Tell me she turned him down. After the confrontation you had with the Newtons, if Ryan thinks Sara's looking into Tabitha's disappearance too, who knows what ulterior motive he might have?"

Kaylee chuckled. "Sara has her own. She said she plans to question him about their prowler and Tabitha."

Jessica winced. "That doesn't sound too safe."

"I agree. I think I'll ask Reese if we can go to the same restaurant tonight to keep an eye on them."

"You're having dinner with Reese?" Jessica asked, her voice going up a few pitches. She cleared her throat. "I mean, that's a good plan."

Kaylee suspected her friend's grin had more to do with the fact that Kaylee was sharing dinner with Reese than that they'd be able to keep an eye on Sara.

After the children had gone home and Sara had left to get ready for her date with Ryan, Jessica reminded Kaylee she'd promised to recount her conversation with Phil. Kaylee twisted Bear's leash in her hand as she debated how much to share.

"You're hesitating," Jessica said. "That can't mean anything good."

Kaylee sighed. "I'm afraid you won't like what he had to say."

Jessica's eyes widened. "They arrested Tabitha?"

"No. Phil still maintains he doesn't know where she is. But

her fingerprints were on the bogus business card Diane Newton claims the female intruder dropped."

Jessica shook her head vehemently. "So I suppose he's convinced Tabitha was the intruder."

"It seems pretty conclusive."

"Someone could be trying to frame her. The real intruder could have gotten Tabitha's fingerprints on the card ahead of time and then worn gloves for the break-in. Did they find her fingerprints anywhere else in the house?"

"Not that he mentioned, no," Kaylee admitted.

"So why would she go to the trouble of wearing gloves to break in if she intended to hand over a card with her fingerprints all over it?"

"It does seem careless, although she could've left the card behind by accident." Kaylee opened the car door for Bear who was tugging on his leash, clearly impatient to get moving.

"You saw Tabitha's house. She is a total neatnik. Carelessness is *not* in her vocabulary," Jessica insisted.

"You still haven't been able to reach Tad?" Kaylee asked, hesitant to drop the bigger bombshell.

"No."

"Well, there's something else." Kaylee stalled, trying to think of a gentle way to express it. Failing that, she decided maybe it was best to come out and say it. "Phil claims Tabitha could be a spy."

"What?" Jessica's gaze flared.

"He claims she changed her name when she came here from Russia," Kaylee rushed on, "and lied about her brother being dead. He's apparently a spy for the Russians, and Phil thinks he convinced Tabitha to access the Newtons' home for them."

Jessica laughed hysterically. "That's the most ridiculous thing I've ever heard," she managed to say when she regained control of herself. "I think your old friend was pulling your leg."

The hairs on the back of Kaylee's neck tingled at the memory of Phil's gun pointed at her windshield. "Trust me. Phil doesn't joke about things like this."

Jessica stopped laughing. "Don't tell me you believe him."

"I don't know what to believe. His argument was pretty convincing. And I got to thinking that maybe the reason Tabitha's date hasn't replied to my e-mails is because her *supposed* date was really her handing off whatever she took from the Newtons' house."

"To her back-from-the-dead brother?" Jessica shook her head, clearly skeptical.

Kaylee thought for a moment, then a course of action came to her. "Reese mentioned that one of his clients was into genealogical research and told him all about it. Maybe he can show me how to dig into Tabitha's family history. If we can track down where she came from and whether or not she had siblings, then at least we'll know if there is any truth to what Phil says."

"Maybe." Jessica defiantly crossed her arms. "I'm sure the NSA can plant whatever information they need to in order to fit the story they want to spin."

Unfortunately, Kaylee didn't have much of an argument for that. She was starting to think Jessica could be right.

Reese arrived at Kaylee's house promptly at six o'clock to pick her up. On the drive over to Tabitha's to feed the cat, Kaylee filled him in on what she'd learned from Phil—minus the NSA agent's scare tactics. Reese didn't need more reason to dislike Phil.

"Well, researching Tabitha's family tree shouldn't be too difficult," Reese said, sounding pleased at the prospect of helping her disprove Phil's claim. "I've already checked out a couple of

the online sites my client showed me. They're pretty thorough."
He parked in Tabitha's driveway. "We can check them out after
dinner if you like."

"That'd be great. Oh, that reminds me, do you mind if we eat
at The Sunfish Café? Sara accepted Ryan's invitation to dinner
there, and I don't trust him."

Reese glanced in the rearview mirror. "If he's driving a black
SUV we'd better hurry. One just zipped by from the direction of
the Newton estate."

"I can be quick." Kaylee jumped out of Reese's truck and
hurried to the backyard. By the time she had fished the key out of
her purse at the door, Reese was at her side, scoping the hedges
surrounding the property.

When she opened the door and no cat came scampering
across the floor to greet her, she remembered that Peony had
gone out that morning. "Do you see the cat?" Kaylee asked Reese.

Reese peered around. "No."

"Here kitty, kitty," Kaylee called to no avail. She groaned.
"Figures she'd pick tonight to play hide-and-seek."

Kaylee hurried to the cupboard where Tabitha stored the cat
food and brought the container to the door, shaking it. The cat
raced across the yard and did her leg-twining routine, purring
thunderously.

"Good girl." Kaylee stooped down and scooped her up to
carry her inside, where she poured her a fresh bowl of food. "I'm
sorry we can't stay now," she cooed, "but I promise I'll come
early tomorrow morning and give you some attention. You poor
thing—you must be so lonely."

Reese glanced into the rooms he could see from the
entranceway. "Don't feel too bad for her. I've read cats sleep
twenty hours a day."

"Really?" Kaylee gave Peony one last scratch on the back of

her neck. "That makes me feel a little better."

By the time Kaylee and Reese arrived at The Sunfish Café, Sara and Ryan were nowhere to be found. Half the place was filled with boisterous children enjoying a birthday party, and the other half was sparsely populated with older couples who didn't seem bothered by the commotion.

"Maybe Sara and Ryan opted to find somewhere else to eat," Reese said. "I can drive past a few of the other restaurants to see if we can spot one of their cars."

Kaylee nodded. "That's a good idea."

They trolled the streets for over half an hour, but they didn't spot Ryan's vehicle.

Kaylee bit her bottom lip. "What if something has happened?"

"Do you have Sara's cell phone number?" Reese asked.

Kaylee chided herself for not thinking of simply calling Sara sooner. She sent her a text, and within a minute Sara replied that she and Ryan were enjoying a lovely dinner in Eastsound.

"She's fine," Kaylee told Reese, glancing at the dashboard clock. "I'm sorry for taking you on a wild goose chase. Now we won't have much time to do the genealogical search."

Reese's answering smile was warm, as if he didn't mind in the least. "What do you say we pick up a pizza and take it back to your place so we can get started on the research?"

Half an hour later, they were settled at Wildflower Cottage's kitchen table with a box of pizza on one side and a laptop on the other, with Reese showing Kaylee the genealogy sites between bites. By the time they were ready for an after-dinner cup of hot cocoa, Reese had found a family record that seemed promising. "Here's a Jenica and Aloysha Petrov," he said.

Kaylee scrunched her forehead, not seeing the connection.

"You said Tabitha's family Bible lists her mother's name as Jane and her father as Al Stone, right?" Reese switched to another tab on the computer browser and pointed out the translations. "Petrov is Russian for 'stone.' Al is short for Aloysha and Jenica is a Russian form of Jane."

"Oh, wow!" Kaylee couldn't help but be impressed by the revelation.

"Do you remember the dates of their deaths?"

Kaylee pulled out the piece of paper she'd jotted them down on. "They match," she said eagerly, then sobered at the realization of what that meant. "So Phil could be right about Tabitha. Do the records show a brother?"

"Yes, an older brother, Gustav. There was also a baby girl born after Tabitha who died shortly after birth."

"Is there a death record or U.S. immigration record for Gustav?"

"No death record." Reese navigated to another site. "And no immigration record for Gustav Petrov, although there are more than a dozen for G. Stone." He scanned the list. "None match or even come close to matching Gustav's age."

"But it doesn't mean he didn't slip into the country on a travel visa, maybe under an assumed name." Kaylee frowned. "It's all speculation on Phil's part. But the NSA must have some intelligence to back up the allegation."

"Intelligence can be misinterpreted." Reese pointed to the screen. "I think I've found Tabitha's immigration record."

Kaylee's heart thumped against her ribs.

"She arrived under the name *Stone* and listed her nationality as Estonian."

"Which was a Russian-occupied country at the time, wasn't it?"

"Yeah." Reese sighed. "Jessica isn't going to be happy to hear this."

Kaylee shook her head. "She won't believe it. She has no doubt the NSA is capable of planting information that serves their purpose."

"And what about you?" Reese asked.

"I still don't know what to think," Kaylee replied. She met Reese's gaze and saw in his eyes the same concern that was in her own mind. "But now I'm a whole lot more worried."

13

"You're not going to believe what I have!" DeeDee exclaimed the next afternoon, rushing into the lighthouse keeper's quarters with her daughters, Polly and Zoe, minutes before the rest of their campers were due to arrive. She waved a flash drive in front of Kaylee, Jessica, and Sara, who were running that afternoon's session while Mary and Gretchen watched The Flower Patch and Death by Chocolate, respectively.

"What?" the trio said in unison.

"Footage of Tabitha in the ferry parking lot the night she disappeared."

Kaylee did a double take. "Seriously?"

"Yes, seriously," DeeDee replied. "One of my regular customers, Carlotta, was in the store picking up a true-crime book about a mysterious disappearance, so I told her about the real-life case right here in Turtle Cove. And she said she saw Tabitha that night. She remembers because a kid on a bicycle swerved in front of her car and then bumped into Tabitha. Carlotta said that by the time she parked, she couldn't find Tabitha to tell her she'd caught it on her dashcam if she wanted the footage."

"What time was that?" Sara asked, appearing as shocked as Kaylee felt.

"A little before six, I think, because Carlotta's sister came in on the late afternoon ferry and Carlotta went to pick her up. I haven't had a chance to look at the footage yet, but I was thinking that as she drove about the lot looking for a parking spot, she might've also captured where Tabitha headed after the incident—and if she was with anyone."

Jessica glanced quickly around the room. "Did anyone bring their laptop?" she asked just as excited children's voices sounded outside the door.

"I did," Kaylee said. "But we'll have to wait until after camp finishes to watch it."

"This is going to be the longest three hours ever," DeeDee predicted.

Fortunately, she was wrong. Once they were all together, the students talked over each other in their eagerness to share how their families had reacted to their stories about eating bugs and stinging nettles. Their enthusiasm was contagious, carrying them all through the afternoon's activities so that the time seemed to fly by. Before Kaylee knew it, parents were back to pick up their children.

When they'd waved goodbye to the last child and Polly and Zoe had gone to entertain Bear out in the yard, Kaylee grabbed her laptop from her car and brought it back into the keeper's quarters. "Okay, let's take a look at what you've got, DeeDee."

Kaylee set the laptop on the table, and they arranged chairs so everyone could see the screen. She plugged in the thumb drive and opened the video file.

"Fast-forward to when she pulls into the ferry parking lot," Jessica said, clearly eager to see the footage.

Kaylee advanced to the point where Carlotta's car steered into the lot.

"There's Tabitha!" DeeDee pointed to a blonde in the distance.

"Is that you talking to her?" Jessica asked Sara. The woman had her back to the camera and wore a hat.

Sara squinted at the screen. "Looks like my coat. It was right around that time I ran into her."

Suddenly a teenage boy on a bicycle swerved in front of Carlotta's car, then barreled toward the two women.

Kaylee barely suppressed a gasp. "He looks as if he's aiming straight for you."

Sara's forehead furrowed. "It's funny, I don't remember that."

At the last second, the kid swerved around them and sped off.

Carlotta must have turned her car in an attempt to keep the boy in view of the dashcam, but three seconds later, he disappeared behind a building. The view then returned to where Tabitha and Sara had been standing.

"It looks like Carlotta backed into a parking spot," DeeDee theorized.

"I've left already," Sara said. "I don't think the kid could've cut as close as the footage makes it look. Tabitha didn't say anything to me about him, and she would've reacted if she'd felt we were in danger. All I remember her worrying about was her date seeing us together before she went into the café. She didn't want him to recognize me" — Sara's voice cracked — "if she gave me the signal to give her an out later. I wish I'd put off my errands and gone to the Sunfish ahead of them. Maybe—" She stopped and put a hand over her mouth, clearly fighting tears.

Jessica patted Sara's arm reassuringly. "Her disappearance isn't your fault."

DeeDee hit pause on the footage. "So, Sara, Jess told me you went out with the admiral's son last night. Did he divulge anything that might be a clue to what happened at Pennybrook Grove Thursday night?"

Sara frowned and shook her head. "He was out for dinner with his dad and his aide when the admiral got the call from the alarm company. Ryan told me he stayed behind and finished his dinner while the other two headed back to the house."

"Did he say where they ate?" Kaylee asked.

"I think he said it was at Filibuster, on the edge of town," Sara answered.

Kaylee nodded. It was the one she'd followed Phil to the previous day, where he'd questioned the hostess. He must have been checking up on what Ryan had done after his father and Shawn had left. Kaylee felt somewhat heartened that at least it seemed as if Phil wasn't taking everyone's alibi at face value. Not that Ryan could've broken into the house, since he had the perfect alibi—being with his dad—but it made her wonder. Had he set it up that way so a cohort could break in, and he just hadn't counted on his mother choosing that evening to arrive?

"I don't think he had anything to do with Tabitha's disappearance," Sara went on. "He didn't quiz me at all about her, or about you for that matter, which I was expecting if he'd been concerned about the questions you asked his mother Monday afternoon."

"That's a relief, I guess," Jessica chimed in.

Sara glanced at her watch. "I'd better get going. I promised my mom I'd make supper for us tonight."

"How is she doing?" Jessica asked. "It's been so long since I've seen her in the bakery. I'd heard she had a lengthy hospital stay this last time."

"It's been a rough couple of years for her," Sara said quietly, "and I'm afraid it's only going to get worse."

"I'm sorry to hear that," Jessica said, and DeeDee and Kaylee added their sympathies as well before Sara left.

After Sara was gone, Kaylee said, "I didn't realize her mom is unwell."

DeeDee nodded. "Sara was Polly's homeroom teacher last year and had to miss quite a few days of work. She's the only family her mother has. Her father died a few years ago, and she has no siblings."

"That's tough." Kaylee gazed out the window, watching Sara's car drive away. "I'm surprised she volunteered to help with the camp if she has so much on her plate. You'd think she would've welcomed the break."

DeeDee shrugged. "Maybe she likes to keep busy. Or she wanted an excuse to have a bit of time out of the house each day."

"What she needs is some time out of the house with people her own age, not just children," Jessica said. "I'm glad she got the chance to go out with Ryan now that we know he isn't unhinged."

"Although he doesn't sound as if he's exactly boyfriend material," Kaylee said. "Phil indicated he's still leeching off his parents."

Polly and Zoe appeared at the door, and Polly asked, "Mom, are you almost done? We're getting hungry."

"We'll only be a few more minutes," DeeDee promised.

"They're welcome to have more of the chocolate muffins I brought for the kids' snack," Jessica said. "If you're not worried it'll spoil their supper."

Zoe and Polly squeezed their hands together and gave DeeDee their best supplicating expressions.

"Oops," Jessica said. "I guess I shouldn't have said it in front of them."

DeeDee laughed. "It's okay. Yes, you can each have one. Then you can run around outside some more to work off the sugar. Got it?"

They squealed in delight and dashed to the box still sitting on a nearby table.

DeeDee returned her attention to the computer. "Okay, let's finish watching this."

Next, Tabitha started walking away from Carlotta's approaching car and, a moment later, a dark-colored sedan pulled up alongside her. Tabitha climbed into the back seat, seemingly of her own free will, and then the car sped off.

"Do you think that was her date?" Jessica asked.

Kaylee shook her head. "If it was, it's weird she climbed into the back instead of the passenger seat, don't you think?"

DeeDee rewound the footage and played it again. "It looks as if there's already someone in the passenger seat."

Jessica reached over and paused the video, then grabbed a pen and notepad from her purse. "Can you make out the license plate number? That'll be the quickest way for us to figure out who's driving the car."

Kaylee and DeeDee squinted at the screen and debated letters.

"Let's try zooming in." DeeDee tapped a few keys.

"That one's definitely an F," Kaylee said.

Jessica jotted down the plate number as they deciphered it, then squinted at the screen. "Hey, what happened to the paper bag she was carrying?"

"What bag?" DeeDee rewound the tape, but there was no sign of a bag in the moments before the dashcam swerved to track the cyclist. She rewound farther.

Jessica pointed to the screen. "There, see? She's carrying a small paper bag in her left hand."

"Play it forward," Kaylee said, watching for the cyclist.

The kid swerved in front and then around past Tabitha's left side, after which the bag was gone.

"The kid took it!" Kaylee exclaimed.

DeeDee played the video again, staring hard at the screen in concentration. "Why didn't Tabitha react? If a kid stole my bag, I'd be yelling 'Stop, thief!'"

Jessica frowned, and Kaylee wondered if she was thinking what Kaylee was thinking—that Tabitha had been expecting the kid or someone else to take the bag. Perhaps it contained something she'd stolen from the admiral's house.

"We should show this to the sheriff," DeeDee said.

"I can do that," Kaylee volunteered. "But first, I'd like to view it a couple more times to make sure there isn't anything else we're missing."

"No problem." DeeDee gathered up her coat and bags. "Unfortunately, I can't stay. Andy and I are going out tonight, so I need to get the girls home and fed."

"Do you have anything else on this flash drive?" Jessica asked.

"I used a blank one to download the dashcam files, so I don't need it back." DeeDee opened the door and called her daughters.

Bear scampered inside and rejoined Kaylee and Jessica.

"How about we take this back to The Flower Patch?" Kaylee suggested to Jessica. "That way Mary can see it too. Maybe she'll spot something we missed."

"Great idea."

A few minutes later, they parked outside The Flower Patch. As they headed inside, Reese came out of Death by Chocolate carrying a cup of coffee. He cocked his head, seeming bemused. "What's up? Did the camp kids run you through the wringer?"

"No, why?" Kaylee asked.

"You both look pretty stressed."

Kaylee and Jessica glanced at each other and burst into laughter at their furrowed brows.

Recovering, Kaylee glanced around and lowered her voice as Reese drew closer. "DeeDee got a copy of surveillance footage from the night Tabitha disappeared, and some things don't quite seem to add up. We're going in to watch it again with Mary."

"Can I join you?" he asked.

"Absolutely," Kaylee agreed readily. "The more eyes the better. I know we should take it to the sheriff, but since the admiral hasn't admitted to local law enforcement that anything was stolen from his house, I doubt he'll appreciate what we think is happening in the video. And I suspect Phil would rather Eddie not see it at all."

"But I'm not sure we should show it to Phil," Jessica interjected. "He'll only see what he wants to see, and that won't bode well for Tabitha."

Kaylee sighed, torn over what to do.

"Sounds as if I need to see the footage to understand what you two are talking about." Reese opened The Flower Patch's front door and held it for them.

The gray cloud Reese had sensed hovering over their heads must have returned and followed them inside, because Mary took one look at them and asked, "What's wrong?"

Jessica filled her in while Kaylee took her laptop out of the bag and set it up on the counter.

"It's five to five and no customers are here," Mary said. "Should I put up the *Closed* sign?"

Kaylee nodded as she plugged in the power cord. "That's a good idea."

Reese squeezed Kaylee's shoulder encouragingly, and only then did she realize how despondent she must've sounded. She knew beyond a doubt that Phil would be furious if she didn't share this footage with him and he learned about it later. But she still didn't feel totally comfortable trusting the agent. Not when he was so convinced Tabitha was a spy and Kaylee wasn't sure she agreed.

Then again, the footage was pretty incriminating.

They all gathered around the computer and watched the footage frame by frame from the beginning. Jessica immediately spotted things they'd missed, or at least hadn't recognized the significance of on their first viewing.

"There's the cyclist," Jessica pointed out. The dashcam had caught the teenager stopped with his bike in front of the drugstore at the parking lot entrance, his gaze directed toward the ferry building, where Tabitha and Sara stood.

The video continued, and Reese and Mary saw why the cyclist was significant.

"Hey, he stole her bag," Reese said immediately.

Mary stopped the playback. "And she didn't react." She frowned at them. "There's no way she could have not felt that. Look." She pointed to Tabitha's hand. "It appears as if she lifted her arm to make it easier for him to swipe it when she realized his intention."

"Which could simply mean she knew better than to risk her life to hang on to something of little value," Jessica argued.

"But with so many people around, it's doubtful she'd have felt in any kind of serious danger," Reese said. "Is that Sara talking to her?"

"Yes," Kaylee confirmed.

Reese rubbed his chin. "Did Tabitha say anything to her about the kid taking her bag? Because you'd think Sara would glance his way, at the very least."

"Sara says Tabitha didn't mention a thing, and Sara doesn't even remember the kid."

"Which makes it seem as if Tabitha was expecting the kid." Reese shot Jessica an apologetic look.

"Or she could've been too stunned to react," Jessica said.

"Let's keep watching." Kaylee resumed the video, hoping to defuse Jessica's rising tension.

"Did you write down the car's license plate number?" Reese asked as Tabitha climbed into the dark sedan on the screen.

"I've got it." Jessica pulled the piece of paper from her purse. "I was thinking Mary could ask her friend at the DMV to trace it."

"Sure." Mary took the paper and pulled out her phone.

"Why not ask Alan Brooks?" Reese asked.

The muscle in Jessica's cheek tensed. "Because then we'd have to tell a sheriff's deputy why we want to know."

"Ah." Reese shot a sympathetic glance at Kaylee.

At least now he understood the corner Kaylee was in. Whatever she did with this footage, someone wasn't going to be happy with her.

"It's a rental car." Mary pointed to the laptop screen with one hand as she put the phone to her ear. "See the sticker on the windshield? All the rentals have those."

"I didn't even notice it," Reese said, sounding impressed.

"Hi, Brenda, this is Mary Bishop," Mary said into her phone. After a few pleasantries, Mary continued, "I was wondering if you could tell me who rented a dark sedan Thursday night?" Mary gave the license plate number, then a moment later she frowned at the phone, clearly disappointed by Brenda's response.

Jessica, Reese, and Kaylee remained silent, but exchanged anxious glances as they listened to Mary's side of the call.

"It's really important," Mary pressed. "No, I understand. Could you at least tell me if the car is still being rented by the same person or if it has been returned already?" Mary was quiet for a moment, then nodded. "Thank you, Brenda. I appreciate your help."

"So, what did she say?" Jessica asked as Mary disconnected the call.

"Whoever rented the vehicle still has it," Mary reported. "And unless Brenda deliberately changed pronouns to throw me off, which I doubt, the renter is a *he*. He rented the car last Wednesday by the week and, as of yet, hasn't returned it."

"So the driver is unlikely an islander," Reese concluded. "At least not a year-round one." He tapped the computer mouse to resume the playback. "Tabitha doesn't hesitate to climb into the car, so she must know the driver."

"I think we should try to check out the license plate on everyone's rentals over at the Newton estate," Jessica said.

"Phil's driving a dark-blue pickup," Kaylee said. She wouldn't soon forget the sight of it gunning toward her on a deserted rural road.

"And his sidekick supposedly didn't get to the island until Friday morning," Reese added.

"Which still leaves the admiral, his aide, and his son," Mary said.

"Ryan has a red sports car," Kaylee said. "But the admiral's aide was driving a dark sedan." Kaylee closed her eyes and tried to picture the license plate from the afternoon she'd seen him at the Pennybrook Grove gate, but she shook her head. "I can't remember the plate number."

"Hey, isn't that the admiral's son?" Mary pointed to the computer screen then quickly tapped the mouse to freeze the frame.

Kaylee gaped at the screen. "It is, and that looks like Sara he's talking to." The time on the bottom of the screen indicated this was now ten minutes later, presumably after Carlotta had collected her sister from the ferry.

"I thought Sara hadn't met him before yesterday," Jessica said.

"Actually, they talked briefly when we were at the estate Monday," Kaylee recalled.

"They sure appear as if they already know each other." Mary tapped the computer mouse once more. The footage resumed and the pair were soon out of view.

They all continued watching until the dashcam caught the *Thank You for Visiting Turtle Cove* sign on Carlotta's way out of town.

Mary stopped the playback. "Well, that raises a whole lot more questions, doesn't it?"

14

For a long moment, Kaylee, Jessica, Reese, and Mary stared at the Turtle Cove visitors' sign still pictured on Kaylee's laptop screen.

Reese finally broke the silence. "I think you need to give this to the sheriff. The rental company will tell him who rented the car that picked up Tabitha. A deputy can question the guy and maybe find Tabitha at the same time."

"Reese is right," Mary agreed. "Tabitha accepted the offered ride without a second's hesitation. There's no reason to think she came to any harm after getting in."

"Except that no one's heard from her since," Jessica argued.

"That's not exactly true," Kaylee said. "She texted Tad."

"Maybe." Jessica tapped the computer mouse to close the video. "Or maybe someone else sent the text. Or maybe whoever took Tabitha got to Tad too, and he lied about receiving a text. Why else would he have suddenly gone silent on me?"

"What do you think we should do with the footage, Jess?" Kaylee asked.

"Keep it under wraps for now," Jessica answered. "At least until we figure out who is driving the rental and maybe watch what he's up to. See if he's acting suspicious."

"Suspicious how?" Reese asked, his rigid posture making it clear he was uncomfortable with the idea of them spying on a potential bad guy.

"Suspicious like he has Tabitha stashed away wherever he's staying," Jessica said.

Reese shook his head. "If that's the case, then it's definitely a job for the sheriff's department."

Jessica sighed. "Fine. Better them than the NSA guys. They already think she's a spy, and if they see this, they're going to be convinced she took something from the admiral's place, handed it off to the kid on the bike, and then made her getaway with the guys in the rental car."

"And what if that's what she did?" Reese asked. His tone was mild, but he still earned a frown from Jessica.

"Sometimes people don't turn out to be who we think they are," Kaylee added softly, and cringed inwardly at the memory of Phil training his gun on her. He definitely wouldn't be happy about her traipsing around the island trying to hunt down the rental vehicle in question.

"We could check the admiral and his aide's license plates first," Mary suggested. "And has Sara seen this footage? She could probably tell us who the kid on the bike is. If he has been in Turtle Cove any length of time, he would've been in her classroom at some point."

"She saw it," Kaylee said. "But she didn't seem to know him."

Mary rewound the footage to an image of the cyclist and printed off his picture. "My neighbor is a high school teacher. Maybe she'll recognize the boy. If I can get his name, then at least we can question him about what was in the bag he lifted. I find it hard to believe a spy ring would risk using a local kid as the go-between."

"Unless he's not a local kid," Reese said.

"With any lucky, we'll know soon enough," Mary said optimistically.

"I can pay the Newtons an impromptu visit when I go to feed Tabitha's cat," Kaylee volunteered. "I'll check the license plate numbers of their rentals while I'm there."

"I'll go with you," Reese said in a tone that indicated it wasn't up for debate.

"Sure. I'd appreciate the company." The truth was, Kaylee didn't want to face Phil again alone, and after what she'd seen on the tape, she was no longer as sure about Tabitha's innocence as Jessica seemed to be.

"I'll ask Sara if she knows why Ryan was hanging around the ferry dock Thursday evening," Jessica said.

"Good plan," Kaylee said. "Okay, let's meet at Death by Chocolate at eight tomorrow morning and compare notes. I'll let DeeDee know."

"See you then. I need to go relieve Gretchen." Jessica grabbed her purse and exited the shop.

"Want a ride home, Kaylee?" Reese asked. "I can pick you up in the morning and bring you back for our meeting at the bakery."

Kaylee suspected the offer was Reese's way of ensuring she didn't go off snooping somewhere on her own this evening, but she was feeling so tired that she was happy to not have to drive. "That sounds great, thanks."

Ignoring Mary's smirk at Reese's offer and her acceptance, Kaylee checked to make sure the shop was ready for the next day, then followed Reese out to his truck.

Bear sat on the front seat between them for the drive. While they headed out of town, Kaylee mentally reviewed whether she had enough food in her refrigerator to invite Reese in for supper.

As if he could read her mind, Reese slowed his truck near the edge of town. "Hungry?" he asked.

"Very," Kaylee admitted.

"Good." He pulled into the parking lot of High Plains, a sit-down burger place.

It wouldn't have been her first choice, but—"Hey, wasn't that the admiral's aide?" She swung around in her seat for a better view, but the man had already walked into the restaurant.

Reese shrugged. "I recognized his car when it passed me

at that last stoplight. I figure we can kill two birds with one stone—feed ourselves and find out if we should be suspicious of what Shawn's up to."

"I knew I kept you around for a reason," Kaylee said teasingly. "But what about Bear?"

"It's a cool evening." Reese rolled his window down a few inches. "He'll be okay in the car, right?"

"Probably. And I think I have a spare rubber bone he can chew on while we're inside." Kaylee quickly fished out the bone and gave it to Bear, then scouted the lot for rental cars. "Which car is his?"

Reese pointed to a black sedan nearby. "The license plate doesn't match the one in the video."

Kaylee blew out the breath she'd been holding, not sure whether to be relieved or annoyed. "Oh well. The food smells good at least."

Inside the restaurant, Reese asked the hostess if they could be seated in the booth directly behind where Shawn sat alone. Reese took the side backing onto Shawn's seat, which meant he wouldn't be able to see anything Shawn did.

Kaylee sat opposite Reese and realized she wouldn't be able to see or hear much from her vantage point either. She leaned across the table and asked, "Wouldn't it have been better to sit in the middle where we could keep an eye on him?"

Reese opened one of the menus the waitress left on the table. "I was thinking it'd be better if he doesn't know we're here."

"Right. Good thinking." Kaylee glanced up and her breath caught. "Someone just joined him," she murmured. "A stocky, dark-haired guy with some kind of tattoo twining around his wrist."

Reese nodded, then said nonchalantly, "What sounds good to you?"

Kaylee scanned the menu. "Cheeseburger and fries with a side salad."

Reese signaled to the waitress and ordered two of the same with water.

Kaylee started to say something, but Reese touched his finger to his lips and tilted his head toward his seat, indicating he was listening in on Shawn's conversation. Kaylee could just barely hear what was being said.

"It needs to be taken care of as soon as possible," Shawn hissed. "Friday at the latest. Can you make it happen?"

"I want half now. Half when it's done," the other man said, his voice husky.

Kaylee glanced at the window. Thanks to the growing twilight, she could make out the man's reflection in the glass.

Shawn's hand slid into view as he pushed a thick envelope across the table toward the stocky man. "Take care of it by tomorrow night and you'll get double."

Kaylee shot Reese a frantic look, but he subtly patted the air with his fingers, cautioning her to play it cool.

"The guy's getting up," Kaylee whispered.

"Stay and have a drink," Shawn said to his companion.

Kaylee shifted toward the edge of the booth for a better view. The man wore scuffed sneakers, faded jeans, and a well-worn leather bomber jacket.

"No time." The man stuffed the envelope into the pocket of his jacket. "I'll be in touch."

"We need to follow him," Kaylee whispered to Reese.

The waitress chose that moment to arrive with their orders.

"Sorry, but can we get some to-go containers? An emergency's come up." Reese pulled his wallet out of his pocket.

"No problem. Let me box up your food."

"That'd be great, thanks." Reese gave her his credit card to pay for the meal and she disappeared.

"We've got to hurry." Kaylee glanced out the window and

saw that the man had already started across the parking lot. "I'll wait for you at the truck," she said, wanting to at least catch some details about his car and see which way he turned out of the lot.

By the time Reese got to the truck with their burgers, the mystery man had already driven off.

"He's in a gray Honda sedan," Kaylee reported. "He turned south back into town."

"Got it." Reese opened the door for her. Once she'd climbed in, he handed her the takeout bag then went around to his side and slid behind the wheel. "Did you get the license plate?"

"Yes," Kaylee said, gently pulling Bear away from the bag of food she'd set on the center console.

"You should call it in."

"And say what? I think the driver of this vehicle is a hit man?" She couldn't keep the exasperation from her voice.

"You do, don't you?" Reese glanced at her.

"Yeah, but for all we know, Shawn hired the guy to buy impossible-to-get Broadway tickets for his mother's birthday."

"Right." Reese caught up to the gray Honda and eased off the accelerator. "Because scalpers always meet their customers in out-of-the-way burger joints."

Kaylee grabbed the dash to brace herself as Reese took a corner a little too fast. "Okay, maybe that was a little ridiculous, but there could be a perfectly logical explanation that doesn't involve anyone getting killed."

"But it's not likely legal either."

Bear whined, clearly not happy about their heated discussion—or maybe just unhappy Kaylee wasn't cracking open the bag of burgers.

"Let's just see where he goes first," Kaylee said. "Okay?"

The man navigated into the ferry parking lot and pulled into line to board the next ferry.

"He's leaving the island," Reese said.

"So does he have Tabitha stashed off island, or did she go into hiding off island and he plans to find her?"

"That's *if* Shawn hired him to deal with Tabitha." Reese parked his truck and stared at the growing line of vehicles waiting to board the ferry. "Maybe we did jump to the wrong conclusion. Why would Shawn want Tabitha dead?"

"If she accessed information she shouldn't have." Kaylee hugged Bear against her chest. "Or maybe Shawn paid her to break in and now that he has what he wants, along with an ironclad alibi, he's tying up loose ends."

Reese glanced at the dash clock. "Do you want to follow him? Chances are we wouldn't make the last ferry back tonight."

"I don't want to let him get away."

"But if he's an assassin, we're not equipped to stop him. We'd be better off telling the sheriff to alert the mainland police."

Kaylee sighed. "Somehow, I think the only person who will take our concerns seriously enough to act on them in time is Phil."

"Do you trust him?"

"I think we're going to have to."

Reese shifted his pickup into park. "Then let's sit here and make sure this guy really does board the ferry, then we'll go feed Tabitha's cat and pay Phil a visit." Reese opened the paper bag he'd brought from the restaurant, and the aroma of fries and burgers filled the cab. "We might as well eat while we wait."

Bear sat up, panting blithely, and Reese tossed him a french fry.

By the time they had finished their burgers and fries, sharing probably more with Bear than was good for him, the line of waiting cars was beginning to crawl toward the yawning stern of the boat.

Once the car behind the Honda had it gridlocked onto the ferry, Reese started his truck. "Okay, we're out of here. Given the time it takes the ferry to get to the mainland dock, Phil should have more than enough time to mobilize a tail to be waiting for this guy."

"As long as we can find Phil." Kaylee fished her cell phone out of her purse and clicked on Phil's number. "I'm going to ask him to meet us at Tabitha's in fifteen minutes."

"Good plan. Less chance the admiral's aide would be alerted that way."

"Or anyone else in that house we might not be able to trust."

At this hour, traffic was light, and Reese made it to Tabitha's in less than ten minutes. They made short work of filling the cat's food, and Kaylee apologized to Peony once more for not having time to give her extra fuss.

Someone hopped over Tabitha's back fence as Kaylee was relocking the back door.

"Who's there?" Reese demanded, yanking up a nearby shovel and wielding it like a bat.

"Shh! It's me, Phil." The NSA agent stepped out of the shadows into the small circle of illumination offered by a lone motion-sensor bulb at the back of the house. "I got the impression you didn't want anyone to know I was talking to you. Was I wrong?"

"No, you're right." Kaylee filled him in on the conversation they'd overheard at High Plains between the admiral's aide and the husky-voiced guy, then she handed him a paper with a description of the car and its license plate number. "We were hoping you could arrange to have someone track him when he gets off the ferry."

Phil shook his head. "I should've known you wouldn't listen to me about not poking around," he growled.

Kaylee's heart dropped. *Is Phil in on this too?*

"Good work," he added begrudgingly, relieving some of her tension. Phil pulled his phone from the case strapped to his hip. "I'll get someone on it right away. Excuse me a minute." He wandered toward a dark corner of the yard as he spoke in quiet tones to whoever was on the other end of the line.

Kaylee's imagination flashed through other scenarios. *What if he's calling someone to arrest us? Or to get rid of us as we leave Tabitha's?* She shook her head vigorously. No, Phil wouldn't do that. She was practically like a sister to him . . . or at least she had been once.

"You did the right thing." Reese squeezed her hand, sending a thrill through her.

"I hope so."

Reese dropped her hand as Phil rejoined them.

"Okay, consider the problem taken care of," the agent said. "Go home and try to forget about what you heard."

"You'll tell us if your colleague finds Tabitha, right?" Kaylee asked, suddenly realizing that if he still believed Tabitha was a spy, their tip may not have spared her at all.

Phil's cheeks filled with air—and seemingly a variety of things he wanted to say—then he slowly exhaled. "I'll tell you what I can, Kaylee. But for your own safety, you do need to leave this alone."

"Can you answer one more question first?" Kaylee asked.

"If I can."

"What are the makes, models, and license plates of the Newtons', Shawn's, and your colleague Mark's rentals?"

Phil squinted at her inquisitively, but he didn't ask why she wanted to know. He recited the makes and models and even the plate numbers, as she'd known he would be able to. He'd always had a photographic memory. It was probably what made him so good at his job.

Kaylee tilted her head. "That's all of them?"

"That's it," he confirmed, which meant it was unlikely anyone staying at the Newton estate drove the car that had picked up

Tabitha from the ferry dock Thursday night.

Kaylee's shoulders sagged in the moment's defeat. *Hopefully Mary had more luck tracking down that kid on the bike.*

15

Kaylee mulled over her mixed feelings about Phil's trust-worthiness as Reese reversed out of Tabitha's driveway.

Suddenly he stomped on the brake. "Did you ever get a response to the e-mail you sent to the date Tabitha was supposed to meet Thursday night?"

"With everything happening, I forgot to check." She opened the passenger door. "I can run back in now and access the account on Tabitha's computer. I could use my phone, but it'd be faster on her laptop."

Reese shifted the truck back into park and trailed Kaylee inside, leaving Bear in the truck.

Kaylee drew the front drapes closed and turned on only a small desk lamp so as not to alert anyone driving by to their presence. She booted up Tabitha's laptop and signed in to the dummy account she'd created. Her spirits spiked when a notice for one new e-mail flashed. "This could be it." At the sight of Ned Banford's name on the sender's line, she gave a fist pump, then clicked the e-mail.

> Ms. Bleu,
>
> I'm sorry, but Tabitha isn't with me. She never showed at the café and didn't call. I assumed she stood me up, although I did check online reports for a couple of days to make sure she wasn't in an accident.
>
> If you think I can be of any more help, I will be coming

in on the early ferry tomorrow. I'm an architect, and I usually pick up coffee at Death by Chocolate before I head to my client's if you want to meet me at the bakery.

Regards,

Ned Banford

"That's convenient," Reese said. "We'll all be there already. Do you have a picture of this guy?"

"No, I couldn't find him online. And even though he walked in front of my car, I think I was too shocked to really register his face."

"May I?" Reese pointed to the desk chair and Kaylee got up so he could sit in front of the laptop. A few clicks later, he had a menu of the images stored on Tabitha's computer. "Nothing here either."

"I guess we'll have to wait until tomorrow to see what he looks like."

"If he shows," Reese said.

"You don't think he will?"

Reese shrugged. "No, he probably will. Especially if he wants us to cross him off our suspect list."

"You still think he could've kidnapped Tabitha? Then why would he answer the e-mail and offer to meet?"

"To throw us off his scent."

Kaylee shivered. "Right. Well, what he doesn't know is we have footage of the car that picked her up at the ferry. If we can figure out a way to see his car, we should be able to tell if he was the driver."

Reese powered down the computer and closed it. "In the meantime, I can make some calls to check his credentials. If he's an architect, some of my clients are bound to have used his services, or maybe know others who have. We'll find out if he's really who he claims to be."

Kaylee and Bear were ready and waiting when Reese arrived the next morning to drive them to their scheduled rendezvous with DeeDee, Jessica, and Mary at Death by Chocolate. She hoped the other ladies had more news to share than she did, and that Ned Banford actually showed. Of course, they'd have to ask every male they didn't recognize if he was Ned since they had no idea what he looked like.

She checked her phone for the umpteenth time. "I still haven't heard from Phil regarding what transpired with the guy we asked him to have followed," she said to Reese as he drove toward town. "And I've already texted him three times." Her insides churned at the thought of Shawn's deadline and the troubling fear of what job he'd hired the guy to do. "What did your clients have to say about Ned?"

"He's legit. Apparently a top-notch architect, though he runs and markets his business under his given name, Edwin."

"Edwin Banford? So that's why he didn't come up in my Internet search." Kaylee groaned inwardly, embarrassed that she hadn't thought to try searching names Ned was short for. "Did you learn anything else?"

"He lost his first wife more than a decade ago. No children."

"Not Russian?"

Reese laughed. "Not that anyone mentioned, no."

"If Tabitha really did break into the admiral's house, perhaps she took advantage of her previously scheduled date to use Ned as a cover. Only something went wrong."

"Something like the admiral's wife catching her in the act?"

"Yeah." Kaylee's heart grew heavier at the thought of telling Jessica about the implications of the conversation they'd overheard last night. She'd hoped to hear from Phil before it came to that.

After a quick stop at The Flower Patch to drop off Bear, she and Reese went to the bakery and found Jessica, Mary, and DeeDee already assembled around a table, coffee mugs in hand.

"We have a lead," Mary said excitedly while Jessica went to get two fresh cups of coffee for them. "I tracked down our cyclist. He said a blonde hired him to grab the bag. He claims he handed it off to an old bag lady, as instructed, in exchange for his payment."

"A bag lady, huh?" Kaylee scrunched her nose. "I've never seen anyone around town that fits that description, so it must have been someone in disguise. Was Tabitha the blonde who hired him?"

Mary shrugged. "He wasn't sure. I told him she was the woman he snagged the bag from, but he said he rode by too quickly to tell. He'd been told to watch for a blonde walking to the ferry with a brown paper bag in her left hand. He said the bag had an electronic tablet in it, so I'm guessing he was paid well for handing it over, or he would've considered keeping it for himself."

"Did you turn him over to the sheriff?" Reese asked.

"For what?" Mary shook her head. "Tabitha never reported being robbed."

The bell above the door jingled, and Kaylee glanced toward it to see if the customer entering could be Ned. Instead, it was her friend Deputy Nick Durham, who waved and shot his trademark grin toward Kaylee's table before getting in line at the counter.

Kaylee returned the wave, then refocused on Jessica, who

had rejoined them. "Jess, what did Sara say about talking to Ryan that night?"

"She says he asked if she knew when the next ferry was leaving and after she told him, he went into his usual flirting routine to try to score a date," Jessica said. "But Sara didn't have time to play the game because she'd promised to back up Tabitha."

"Or so she thought," DeeDee chimed in.

"Sara didn't clue in that he was connected to the break-in at the Newtons' until he pulled the same routine on her outside the lighthouse the other day and didn't even seem to realize it wasn't the first time he'd tried to pick her up." Jessica helped herself to one of the muffins she'd set out in the middle of the table and then pushed the plate toward Kaylee. "What about you? Did you get a lead on the license plate?"

"Only that the car hasn't been rented to anyone at the Newton estate." The door to the shop opened again and a handsome middle-aged man strode in. Recognizing him as the man she'd nearly run over, Kaylee sprang up and approached him. "Excuse me, but are you Ned Banford?"

Momentarily confused, the man hesitated before finally saying, "Yes I am. Do I know you?"

"My name is Kaylee. I'm the one who sent you the e-mail about watching Tabitha's cat. Do you have a few minutes to chat?"

After the slightest reluctance, Ned sat with Kaylee at a small table and listened while she explained about Tabitha's disappearance and her decision to contact him in case he knew anything that could help.

"Here I thought she stood me up," Ned said when Kaylee had finished. "But she disappeared into thin air. Do the police think her car went off the road or something?"

"No, the sheriff's department located her car, but no one has heard from Tabitha since shortly before her scheduled date with you, when she got into a car at the ferry port."

Ned's head snapped up. "So you assumed she must be with me."

Kaylee shrugged. "It seemed the most logical conclusion."

"I never met her that night," he reiterated. "I have no idea what could've happened to her."

Scrutinizing his profile, Kaylee was nearly certain he hadn't been in the car that had picked Tabitha up.

Ned gave Kaylee his business card. "I need to meet a client, but please call me if you hear from Tabitha. Or if there's anything I can do to help find her."

Kaylee thanked him and rejoined her friends.

While she'd been talking to Ned, Reese had filled them in on how they knew he'd be here and on the conversation they'd overheard the night before between Shawn and his hired gun. Jessica's face had turned a sickly gray, but Kaylee was grateful Reese had spared her from having to break the news to her friend.

"You're sure Ned didn't have anything to do with Tabitha's disappearance?" Jessica asked after Kaylee reported on her conversation with Ned.

"As sure as I can be," Kaylee answered.

"I snapped his picture while you were talking to him," Reese said. "I figured we could show it to the waitress at The Sunfish Café to see if she recognizes him."

"Good thinking," DeeDee said.

"And I think we'd better enlist the sheriff's department's help in getting the car rental company to release the name of the guy driving the car that picked Tabitha up Thursday night," Reese continued. "With any luck, maybe we can locate her before Shawn's guy or whoever Phil enlisted to follow him."

Nick sidled up to their table sipping a coffee. "Did I hear you say you need the sheriff's department's help?"

"Actually yes, and you'd be the perfect man for the job,"

Kaylee said. "Nobody has heard from Tabitha Mason since last Thursday, when someone picked her up in a rental car with this license plate number at the ferry lot." She showed him a piece of paper with the tag number and car's description written on it. "But the rental company won't tell us who rented it, let alone his contact information."

"And is this the same Tabitha Mason reported missing, then reported to be visiting her sister?" Nick asked, but his tone made it sound as if the question was rhetorical. He took the piece of paper. "Let's take a walk down to the rental lot and see if we can change their mind, shall we?"

"Actually, I need to open The Flower Patch," Kaylee said reluctantly.

"Go on. I'll open the shop," Mary said.

Kaylee grinned at the rest of the group and hurried after Nick, retrieving Bear from The Flower Patch on her way out so he could get a quick walk.

Thankfully, the receptionist at the rental car counter was a young woman who, by the way her eyes lit up when Nick walked in, had an affinity for men in uniform, especially those as naturally flirtatious as Nick. In no time, Nick had the information Kaylee was after.

Reading over the paper he handed her listing the client's name, Jonah Kaplan, and temporary address at the Turtle Cove Inn, Kaylee said, "I can't thank you enough."

"Do you want me to go along with you to talk to this guy?" Nick asked. "I'd normally tell you not to investigate these things on your own, but I know that's wasted breath."

She was about to welcome his company when Phil pulled into the rental car lot. She should've known her query about the Newton household's license plates would eventually lead him here. "You know, Nick, I think I can handle it from here. But thanks."

"No problem." Nick took a drink from the coffee he still held. "I'd better get back to my patrol. See you later, Kaylee."

Phil waited for the deputy to stride out of earshot, then approached Kaylee and yanked the slip of paper from her hand. "You promised me you'd stop with the sleuthing."

She grabbed it back. "And you promised me you'd keep me updated on what you found out about Shawn's mystery associate."

Phil clasped Kaylee's upper arm, and Bear growled.

"It's okay, Bear," Kaylee soothed as Phil steered her away from passersby to a quiet spot along the rocky shore.

"You'll be happy to know your overactive imagination blew Shawn's dealings way out of proportion," Phil finally said when they stopped. "He hired that guy to create a diversionary story to wag the dog."

"Wag the what? What are you talking about?"

"It turns out Shawn is convinced the admiral's son orchestrated the break-in to get his hands on something lucrative to sell while giving himself a perfect alibi. And Shawn was afraid it was only a matter of time before the government officials that appointed his boss to his new post figured it out and decided a man who couldn't control his own son wasn't fit to lead an entire fleet."

Kaylee mulled over the information for a moment. "He hired the goon to cause another problem that would keep those officials occupied far away from the admiral."

"Bingo."

"So Tabitha isn't in danger."

"Not from Shawn. I don't know what to think about Ryan. There's no evidence to link him to the robbery, or Tabitha for that matter, but Shawn is still convinced he's behind it somehow."

Kaylee shivered, remembering how Ryan had spied on them at the lighthouse keeper's quarters the day after she'd confronted his mother with her questions. "I remember seeing Shawn and

Ryan arguing on the street one day. That must've been what Shawn was confronting him about. Ryan had just been meeting with a known bookie's daughter, and if he's got a gambling problem, I can see why Shawn would be worried about how low Ryan might stoop to pay it."

Phil nodded. "He does like to gamble."

Kaylee revisited the theory she'd contemplated a few days earlier. "So what if he enlisted a girlfriend to burglarize his folks' place while he was out for dinner with his dad, and she told him Tabitha saw her? Ryan could've been worried Tabitha would ruin his plan and decided to . . ." She couldn't bring herself to finish the sentence.

"Except Tabitha's fingerprints were found in the house."

"But only on a business card, which the other girl could've planted. She must have been wearing gloves if no other fingerprints were found, right?"

"But like I said, no matter how much of a slimeball the guy seems sometimes, there's no evidence to link Ryan to any of it." Phil flicked his finger at the piece of paper Kaylee still held. "Now do you mind telling me the significance of this?"

Kaylee reluctantly filled him in on how they had gotten the license plate number and that it belonged to the vehicle that picked Tabitha up from the ferry lot the last night she was seen.

Phil immediately put in a call to his office to run a background check on the name. Then he relieved Kaylee of the slip of paper. "I'll check it out."

She snatched it back yet again. "Not without me you won't."

He stared her down as if he actually thought he could change her mind. Finally he said, "Fine. We'll do this another way."

He escorted her back to the car rental office. After flashing his identification badge, he convinced the receptionist to locate the car's current position using its GPS tracking system.

The receptionist tapped a few keys and then stared at the screen, her brow furrowed, as she attempted a few more key strokes. "That's strange. The GPS system must be broken. It's not showing the car anywhere."

Phil thanked her and escorted Kaylee out.

"What's going on?" Kaylee asked, keeping her voice low. "Do you think an NSA mole has her? Who else would know how to disable the car's GPS system?"

"You'd be surprised," Phil said, his tone clipped. "But a Russian spy, for one."

Kaylee frowned. "You still think Tabitha is a spy?"

He opened the passenger door of his truck and motioned for her to get in. "I need you to show me the dashcam footage."

Kaylee scooped Bear onto her lap. "Aren't we going to go to the inn and see if these guys have Tabitha there?"

"Not until we know who we're dealing with."

They drove the few blocks to The Flower Patch in silence, and Phil parked in the rear lot. They entered through the back door, Bear trotting ahead to greet Mary.

"Where's your computer?" Phil asked.

"In my office upstairs." Kaylee indicated the steps to the second floor as she walked into the shop's sales floor, where Mary was at the counter with Bear. She introduced Phil, then briefly filled Mary in on what they were doing. "I'll be back down in a few."

"Take your time," Mary said, although she gave Phil a fleeting, skeptical glance. When Kaylee was halfway up the stairs, Mary added, "Reese popped over to The Sunfish Café after we left Death by Chocolate. He showed Ned's picture to the waitress, and she confirmed he was the guy hanging around Thursday night."

"Thanks for letting me know. Where is Reese now?" Kaylee was mildly surprised—and perhaps a little disappointed—that he hadn't waited for her. "He had to get to a job." Mary bent to scratch Bear behind the ears. "Who's a good boy? Do you deserve a treat?"

While Mary spoiled Bear, Kaylee showed Phil up to her office. He took a call on his cell phone as the computer booted up. His grimace told her he wasn't happy about whatever the person on the other end of the phone was saying.

A moment later, he disconnected the call and stuffed it back in its holder. "Our car renter used an alias. Jonah Kaplan doesn't exist."

"That's not so surprising, is it?"

"It's a new identity, but one he backstopped very well."

"Backstopped?"

"Set up a paper trail so someone looking into his background would find a credible history and not realize the guy wasn't real," he explained.

"If it's so credible, how did your people figure out it was phony?"

Phil expelled a pent-up breath. "Because they know what to look for. This was an agency-created alias."

"Agency-created? You mean NSA?"

"If it was NSA, it's top secret, because we're not finding an internal paper trail. More likely it's FBI or DEA. Even CIA isn't outside the realm of possibility."

"I thought they couldn't operate inside the States."

"Yeah, well, rules get broken." He scrubbed his chin. "Of course, it could be the SVR."

"What's that?"

"The modern-day version of the KGB operating outside of Russia. It arguably has more far-reaching power than the old order."

Kaylee's breath caught in her throat. She'd had no idea such an agency even existed. No wonder Phil was so freaked out over Tabitha's Russian heritage. Her family history could very well pose an immediate threat.

16

Kaylee eventually convinced Phil to let her tag along when he went to the Turtle Cove Inn, her main argument being that she'd have followed him otherwise. He hadn't gleaned any more clues than Kaylee and her friends had from viewing Carlotta's dashcam footage, so interrogating the car's driver felt like their last hope.

"Hello, Kaylee," Brian Cook, the manager of the Turtle Cove Inn, said warmly. Kaylee regularly delivered flower orders to the inn, so he knew her well. "What brings you here today?"

Phil flashed his NSA identification. "Phil Haynes, NSA. Could you please tell me what room Jonah Kaplan is staying in?"

Brian eyed Phil skeptically. "I'm not sure I should."

"Please, Brian," Kaylee said. "It could be a matter of national security."

"If you can vouch for him, I suppose I can tell you," Brian replied. "Mr. Kaplan is in room six, but I haven't seen him go in or out since Thursday."

"Has housekeeping been inside his room?" Kaylee asked.

"I'm not sure if Patty has been in there, but we can go ask her. I think she's working on that set of rooms now." Brian walked them down a hallway to room six, where a housekeeping cart was blocking the open door.

Kaylee peered around the cart. The room was empty. No luggage sat on the rack. No shoes sat on the boot mat. No jackets hung in the closet.

Was this why the GPS couldn't locate the vehicle? Had they collected Tabitha and taken her off island?

An older woman in a maid's uniform appeared from a supply closet holding two boxes of tissues. She froze when she saw Kaylee, Phil, and Brian gathered outside room six.

"When is the last time this room was slept in?" Phil asked.

Patty glanced at Brian, who nodded his permission for her to answer. "Last Wednesday night. Everything was gone Thursday morning, but they didn't check out."

"Did they forget?" Kaylee asked.

Patty shook her head. "They prepaid and told the front desk they'd be away a few days, but that they'd be back. They only prepaid through last night, though, which is why I'm cleaning now. We have new guests checking in later."

"They?" Phil repeated. "How many were there? Can you describe them?"

"Two men in their midthirties and well-dressed, in suits and ties."

Phil nodded and thanked her for her help.

"What do you think?" Kaylee asked Phil as they left the inn.

"It doesn't feel right," he said. "If they were Russian spies, they'd hightail it out of here as soon as they had what they'd come for."

"That's exactly what they did. You don't really think they'll come back, do you? They probably caught the next ferry off the island. They paid for their rental for the week and disabled the GPS, so they must've figured no one would be looking for it for at least a week. And they wouldn't have worried about racking up extra charges on their credit card since it was under a bogus name anyway." Kaylee winced, because it was looking more and more as if these men were enemies of the state and, from all appearances, Tabitha had been complicit with them. "They could've blackmailed Tabitha into cooperating with them."

Phil opened his passenger door for Kaylee, then smiled down

at her. "I love the way you're able to imagine a dozen different scenarios for how a crime could've gone down and still manage to think the best of the suspects."

"My friend Jessica believes in Tabitha. And she may be a bit of a conspiracy theorist, but she's always been a good judge of character."

Phil closed her door, then walked around the car and climbed into the driver's seat. "Clearly she is. She's befriended you."

Kaylee shook her head. "Flattery is not going to convince me to stop looking for Tabitha, if that's what you're hoping."

"It never crossed my mind." Phil drove her back to The Flower Patch and parked in the rear lot. "I will let you know if I learn anyone in the agency has Tabitha," he promised. "Hold on, I'll get your door." He hopped out of the truck and hurried around to her side.

"Thank you," Kaylee said as she climbed out.

At the sound of a nerve-shattering crack, she instinctively ducked.

"Look out!" Phil tackled her to the ground a second before a massive tree branch crashed beside them.

Phil crouched beside her and checked her over anxiously. "Are you okay?"

Kaylee's heart raced. "I'm . . . I'm okay." She swallowed hard at the sight of the heavy branch now lying where she'd been standing only a moment earlier.

"Looks as if it was rotted through." Phil gently stroked the hair back from her face and looked so deeply into her eyes that, for a moment, Kaylee thought he might kiss her. Finally he said, "It looks like an accident. Not sabotage."

Sabotage? The possibility hadn't occurred to her, but clearly it had been his worst fear.

He stood and offered her a hand. "I wish I was on vacation."

"Why?" Kaylee asked as he drew her to her feet. She winced at a twinge in her ankle, then swiped the dirt from her torn pants.

"Because I think I've made a big mistake all these years in only letting myself think of you as my kid sister's sidekick."

Kaylee stopped midswipe and gazed up at him, her cheeks heating. Twenty years ago, she would've been putty in his hands at that declaration. But now . . .

From the corner of her eye, she caught sight of people dashing out the side door of Death by Chocolate. She straightened and turning their way, her first thought was she hoped Reese wasn't among them, and that he hadn't seen how Phil had saved her—or how he'd looked at her afterward.

At the sight of Reese leading the charge, her heart thundered.

"She's okay," Phil assured the group. "Nothing to see here."

She smiled her thanks for their concern, said goodbye to Phil, and did her best not to hobble on her sore ankle as she made her way to The Flower Patch's back door.

Once inside, she said to Mary, "I need a few minutes alone, okay?"

Mary glanced from the torn fabric at Kaylee's knee to the ankle she was babying. "What happened?"

"I'll explain. Just give me a few moments." Kaylee started up the steps, leaning heavily on the handrail, with Bear at her feet.

"Can I bring you some ice?" Mary called after her.

"Yeah, that might be good," Kaylee said. "Thanks."

At the sound of the back door creaking open, her heart thumped and she awkwardly quickened her limping pace. She wanted it to be Reese and was worried it was Phil, but whoever it was, she wasn't ready to face him.

"How is she?" Reese's familiar voice traveled up the stairs.

"Shaken up," Mary said. "What happened?"

Desperate to know what he'd seen, Kaylee edged around

the corner at the second-floor landing so she could eavesdrop.

Bear sat on the landing in plain view from the first floor and gazed at her curiously. She motioned him to come to her, but he only tilted his head the other way.

"Get over here," she whispered urgently.

"It's my fault," Reese was saying. "I'd been meaning to cut down the rotted branch on that old tree behind the shop for months." His voice trembled. "It finally gave way and almost crushed Kaylee."

Mary gasped.

"Luckily her friend acted fast and got her clear." Reese's annoyed tone didn't match his words, and a smile tugged at the corners of Kaylee's mouth.

Bear yipped.

"Hush!" Kaylee whispered urgently, reaching out from her hiding place to drag the little dog behind the wall with her.

"I guess you wish it had been you," Mary said gently.

Reese let out an anguished groan. "What am I doing? Ever since my ex broke our engagement, I've been too afraid of getting my heart stomped on again to see what's right in front of me. But I can't ignore it anymore."

Kaylee's heart ached for the anguish Reese must have felt when his former fiancée had left him to "find herself." He'd never mentioned the woman by name, so Kaylee had thought he was over her. Apparently it had been the opposite.

"Ignore what?" Mary asked, though her knowing tone indicated that the question was for Reese's benefit instead of her own.

Reese sighed. "Even I know I'm a fool for not admitting how much I care about Kaylee."

"Let alone *tell* her," Mary added, and Kaylee's heart tripped over a beat or three.

"Yeah." Reese sounded utterly defeated. "And now I'm afraid it might be too late."

"It's never too late," Mary said brightly, and Kaylee could've hugged her. Instead she inwardly squealed and hobbled the rest of the way to her office to change.

What seemed like an eternity later, Mary appeared at the office door with an ice pack. "How's the ankle?"

"Sore," Kaylee said. "Did Reese leave?"

Mary's eyes twinkled. "I did suggest he deliver the ice, but he wasn't sure you'd want to see him."

"I'm not attracted to Phil," Kaylee said.

Mary handed her the ice. "I know."

"Thanks for trying to talk some sense into Reese."

"I thought you might have heard that." Mary peered at her. "Is it time for me to talk some sense into you too?"

"Haven't you been trying to do that ever since I moved back here?" Kaylee joked.

"Yes, but that was teasing," Mary said. "This is serious. He's finally accepting that he has real feelings for you, Kaylee, and I think you feel the same. Maybe it's time to come clean to each other."

Kaylee sighed. "I'm over forty and I've never had a romantic relationship work out. Why should I think one with Reese would be any different? Why jeopardize our friendship for a maybe?"

"Well, my dear." Mary tapped Kaylee's chin. "Some leaps of faith are worth taking."

Mary took over Kaylee's duties at the spring break camp that afternoon while Kaylee stayed at the shop to rest her ankle. Mary also volunteered to fill Jessica and DeeDee in on what had transpired at the rental car agency and the Turtle Cove Inn—news Kaylee hadn't been looking forward to breaking to Jessica.

As the afternoon wore on with only three customers to interrupt her thoughts, Kaylee secretly hoped Reese might stop by to check on her.

He never did.

Of course, Kaylee reminded herself that he'd assume she was with the kids at the camp. But it didn't offer her as much comfort as it should have.

Just after closing time, Mary rushed into the shop while Kaylee was sweeping the sales floor. "Jessica wants us all at the lighthouse in twenty minutes."

"Why?" Kaylee asked. "What's going on?"

"She didn't say, just that it's very important." Mary stooped to hold the dustpan for Kaylee. "Half an hour ago, she got a cryptic message on her phone and had to rush out. She wouldn't tell us where she was going, but she made us promise we'd be there when she got back and that we'd fetch you."

Kaylee grabbed her coat and carefully slid her sore foot into a boot, grateful the swelling had gone down and the pain had almost completely subsided. Kaylee snapped on Bear's lead. "Okay, I'm ready."

Mary drove, and by the time they reached the lighthouse, Jessica's car was in the parking lot. She appeared at the door and motioned them inside, then closed the door and turned the lock behind them.

"I'd like you to meet Tad Mason." Jessica pointed to a young man sitting at a table with DeeDee.

He stood and shook hands as Jessica introduced Mary and Kaylee. "I apologize for the secrecy," he said, "but it's important no one else knows I'm here."

Kaylee's chest tightened. She didn't like keeping secrets,

especially ones that might compromise national security. "Why?" she asked, taking a seat opposite his. "I mean, first you ask us to find your mother. Then you lie to us about where she is. Then you cut off all communication for days."

"Yes, and I'm sorry," Tad said, sounding genuine. "I'm here to explain. You see, federal agents picked me up in DC and interrogated me about my mother. Although they didn't come right out and say it, I got the distinct impression they suspected her of being a spy. No doubt because of her Russian heritage. I was afraid if you all kept searching for my mom, their suspicions about her being a spy might get out."

"It never occurred to you we'd attempt to verify the aunt story?" Kaylee asked skeptically.

"I didn't have much time to think about what to write. I knew the agents would read my texts, so I had to be careful what I wrote."

Kaylee exchanged a look with each of her friends, attempting to gauge whether they believed him. It was plausible, but how could they know for sure? "What kind of federal agents picked you up?"

"NSA."

Kaylee grimaced. So Phil had lied to her. Or someone was keeping him in the dark.

Or Tad was lying.

"They took my phone soon after I sent the text," Tad went on. "And I didn't get the follow-up texts from Jessica until they returned it to me yesterday afternoon."

"How do you know they didn't follow you here?" Mary asked.

"I don't for sure, but I bought a ticket to Florida and had a friend of a friend buy a ticket to Seattle and once we were through security, we exchanged tickets and I gave him my phone." A smile of satisfaction played at the young man's lips. "I figured they'd probably bugged it and were tracking it, so I thought I'd let him lead them on a merry chase through the Everglades."

"Was your uncle a spy?" Kaylee asked.

Tad stiffened, the smile fading. "I have no idea. As far as I knew, he died before I was born."

Kaylee didn't want to pose the next question, but she did it anyway. "Do you think your mom could be working for the Russians?"

"No!" Tad shook his head vigorously. "But I've been around DC long enough to know that if they deem it in their best interest, they'll fabricate stories or create crises to divert political attention away from something they can't afford to be exposed."

"I'm sorry, but I had to ask," Kaylee said. "Tabitha's fingerprints were on the business card found on the Newton estate."

"I've been thinking about that," DeeDee interjected. "Diane didn't mention the business card until days later, right? After she rooted through Tabitha's house . . . or at least so it seemed by the cat hair on her slacks, right?"

"True," Kaylee said.

"So maybe she lifted it from Tabitha's house and made up the story about Tabitha dropping it."

"I guess that's possible." Kaylee frowned. "Except what would be her motive?"

DeeDee scrunched her lips. "I haven't figured that part out yet."

"An NSA agent could've convinced her to produce it," Tad suggested. "To give them grounds to arrest my mom."

"I hate to ask this," Kaylee said, "but many a leader has been felled by romantic indiscretions. Do you think it's possible your mom could've been romantically involved with someone in the Newton household?"

"I can't see it." Tad sighed. "But then again, I didn't know she was seeing a guy she was talking to online either." He raked his fingers through his hair. "I need to go to the house and look around. There's got to be some clue we're missing."

17

Although Kaylee would typically be first in line to hunt for more clues, her aching ankle convinced her to let Jessica take Tad to his mother's house and feed the cat.

During the drive to Wildflower Cottage, Kaylee's mind replayed the day's events and stalled on the memory of Phil reviewing Carlotta's dashcam footage. She was a little surprised he hadn't asked for a copy since he likely had access to sophisticated face-recognition software that could've produced more leads. Then again, maybe he already knew who he was dealing with. The thought irritated her, but she understood that the nature of his job meant that he couldn't always share what he knew.

Convinced there was something she was missing, Kaylee made herself soup and salad and ate it in front of the computer as she rewatched the dashcam footage. There had to be something she was missing. She thought of the cyclist Jessica had spotted several frames before he rode by Tabitha. If the men in the car had been waiting to collect her, then they must've been waiting nearby too. Kaylee rewound the video to a minute before Carlotta reached the ferry lot.

As Carlotta's car slowed at the entrance to the parking lot, Kaylee's breath caught. "That's the car!" The dark sedan was stopped in the traffic lane facing Carlotta, waiting for an opportunity to turn left. Kaylee rewound the footage and watched it again, pausing the film on the image of the car. "There's only one guy in the car." She squinted at the license plate number. "It's the same car. So when does he pick up the second guy?"

Kaylee advanced the footage at half speed, but the next time the car came into view, it already had a second person in the front seat. "That means the driver stopped and picked him up somewhere between the street and this point," Kaylee mused aloud, as she rewound the footage once more.

There were several males heading through the lot to the ferry as Carlotta drove past. Kaylee paused on one in a suit who was standing still. Kaylee mentally pictured the layout of the parking lot. The guy could definitely have been watching Tabitha.

Kaylee continued to watch the footage, holding her breath as she waited to see if the suit-clad man's position would come back into view. It did, but the man was gone. In the next frame, Carlotta had made a sharp correction and caught the sedan, now with a man in the passenger seat, collecting Tabitha.

Kaylee rewound the video to the image of the man in the suit and then called Phil, who said he'd be there in ten minutes.

Five minutes later a knock sounded at the door.

"That was fast," Kaylee said as she yanked it open. But it was Reese, not Phil, who stood on her doorstep.

"You were expecting someone else?" he asked.

Her heart sank. Given what she'd overheard at the flower shop earlier, he would not take well to hearing Phil was on his way over. She reached for his arm and tugged him inside. "Yes, but I'm so glad you're here. I just discovered a huge clue in Carlotta's dashcam footage. I think. Come see."

Not letting go of his arm, she led him to her computer and showed him the image.

"I spotted Tabitha's getaway car first turning into the ferry lot with no passenger. Then I saw this guy." She pointed to the screen. "Unlike everyone else heading to the ferry, he's just standing there, watching someone or something. Then a few frames later, he's disappeared, but now there's a passenger in the car."

"Wow, good work," Reese said. "Phil should be able to run

this guy's image through face-recognition software to see if he's in the system."

"Yeah, I just called to let him know. He's coming over to pick it up."

Reese fell silent and nodded. He backed away from the computer. "I guess I'd better go."

"Please stay." Kaylee placed a hand on his arm. "The truth is, Phil makes me kind of nervous, and I'd feel better if you stayed."

Reese's eyes brightened. "Then of course I'll stay. Are you sure you trust—"

The sound of the doorbell cut short Reese's question.

Kaylee let Phil in. Was the flicker of disappointment in his face when he spotted Reese her imagination? She led him to her computer and ran through the same explanation she'd given Reese.

"Interesting," Phil said.

"Do you think you'll be able to ID this guy?" Kaylee asked.

"I don't need to. I already know who it is. FBI Special Agent Chris Jones."

"How can a federal agent have Tabitha and you not know about it?" Reese asked. "Don't government agencies talk to each other?"

"Not if we can help it," Phil deadpanned. He squinted at the screen. "I should've spotted the covert behavior a mile away. I suspected we were dealing with FBI agents when my office told me Jonah Kaplan was an alias. But what are they investigating? It can't be a robbery that happened less than thirty minutes before this footage was taken."

"Maybe this whole thing is some sort of sting operation," Reese theorized.

Phil nodded. "I hope so, because I know this guy personally, and I'd hate to have to arrest him for working the wrong side of the law." He tapped a key to close down the video playback and ejected the flash drive. "I'm going to have to take this."

Kaylee didn't argue. She doubted there was anything more she could learn from it.

After Phil let himself out, Kaylee called Jessica. "Phil identified one of the men that picked up Tabitha. Apparently, he's an FBI agent."

"Are you serious?" Jessica practically yelped. "Do you think that means she's okay?"

"There's a good chance of that," Kaylee said.

"Unless the agent is crooked," Reese muttered.

Kaylee flashed him a reproachful glare. There could be all kinds of reasons why Tabitha hadn't been allowed to contact her son or friends. She might be in witness protection or, as Reese had said earlier, part of some kind of sting the feds couldn't risk jeopardizing.

"She was blackmailed," Jessica blurted out, then lowered her voice to a whisper. "We shouldn't talk on the phone. I'll be right over."

Ten minutes later, a light tap sounded on Kaylee's back door. Jessica and Tad stood outside, cowering in the shadows.

"Why didn't you come to the front door?" Kaylee asked.

"We don't want anyone to see Tad," Jessica answered.

"Reese is here," Kaylee said as she ushered them in.

"That's fine. We can trust him," Jessica said as much to Kaylee as to Tad.

Kaylee invited everyone to take seats in the living room, then hurried to the kitchen to make cups of cocoa. She returned with a tray and handed out mugs, then asked, "Now what's this about blackmail?"

"I have a secret spot under a floorboard in my room where I always kept treasures as a kid," Tad explained. "My mom knew about it, of course. On a whim, I checked it when we were at the house, and there was a letter from her inside. She must've figured it was the only place she could leave a note I'd find before anyone else."

"And the note said someone blackmailed her?" Kaylee prompted.

"Yes, into stealing something from the admiral's safe. The blackmailer said if she didn't do it, news of her brother being a Russian spy would leak out and my future would be ruined." Tad's voice grew mournful. "She wrote that if I found this letter, she'd had to go into hiding and will try to contact me when it's safe." He let out a ragged sigh. "Whatever she did, she did for me. To ensure I'd have a future." Tears pooled in the corners of his eyes and he pressed at them with his knuckles. "It's not fair. She's a good person. She'd never willingly do something illegal."

Jessica wrapped an arm around his shoulder and squeezed. "It's going to be okay," she promised. "We'll find her."

"If the letter can be believed," Reese said.

"What do you mean *if*?" Jessica shot back.

Reese lifted his hands in surrender. "All I'm saying is the letter gives the impression her blackmailer was a Russian agent, or at least someone familiar with her family history. It doesn't seem to jibe with the fact that an FBI agent picked her up."

Tad's expression suddenly brightened. "Unless she contacted them after the blackmailer recruited her. That's what she could've meant about going into hiding."

"That must be it," Kaylee said. "My friend is going to try and contact the agent we saw in the surveillance footage. I'm sure we'll have answers soon."

A broad smile spread across Jessica's face and she gave Tad another sideways hug. "Hopefully by morning this will all be behind you. C'mon, let's head back to my place. Mila will be wondering what happened to us." To Kaylee, Jessica added, "I asked Mila to cook supper since we'd be late getting back." She lowered her voice for Kaylee's ears only. "I also thought they might enjoy seeing each other again." Jessica added a wink and steered Tad back out through the rear door.

"Why the long face?" Reese asked after Kaylee locked the door behind them.

"I hope Jessica isn't getting her hopes up too much."

"About Mila and Tad getting back together?"

"That too, but more about Tabitha. For all we know, Tad could've planted the note he claims to have found in his secret hiding place."

Reese tilted his head. "You're not usually this cynical about people. Are you sure Phil's suspicions aren't rubbing off on you?"

"Ha, maybe. I just don't want to see Jessica hurt." Kaylee tracked her friend's taillights as they disappeared down the road. "A few days ago, Phil made a comment about people not always being what they seemed, and I took it as a reference to one of his own team or someone close to the admiral. But what if Tabitha was really a sleeper agent and left the letter to keep her son in the dark about her true loyalties?"

Reese curled his arm around Kaylee's shoulder. She hadn't realized how chilled she felt until his warmth seeped into her. "You can't change what's done. All you can do is be there for your friend when she needs you."

Kaylee managed a wobbly smile. "Thanks for being here for me."

He pulled her into an embrace. "There isn't any place I'd rather be."

Kaylee's heart raced as she tipped back her head to gaze into his eyes.

His gaze dropped to her lips. And then . . .

Bear released a series of rapid-fire barks and rapped his paws against the front window.

Reese dropped his arms and turned to the dog. "What is it, boy? What do you see?"

Kaylee's heart pounded for a whole different reason. Was someone prowling outside her house? Had someone followed Tad here?

Reese peered out the window, then yanked on his coat. "I'll check the yard. Lock the door behind me."

"Be careful." Kaylee clicked the lock into place after Reese stepped out. She took up a spot to the side of the window, where she could peer out but not be easily seen. She picked up a still-yapping Bear. "Shh, Bear. Reese is on it." She hugged the little dog to her to fight the chill that had gripped her.

What seemed like an eternity later, Reese knocked on the door. "It was an opossum. I saw him on top of your trash cans before he ran off."

Kaylee's pent-up breath left her in a rush. "Figures."

"I should go now." Reese suddenly sounded shy as he fumbled in his pocket for his keys. "I'll catch up with you at the shop in the morning, okay?"

"Okay. Thank you, Reese." She held the door between them and leaned her head against the side of it. "For everything."

Reese smiled, a twinkle in his eye. "Any time."

The next day, Kaylee dropped Bear off at The Flower Patch and then went straight to Death by Chocolate. Tad was there sitting at a small table, smiling at Mila, who was refilling his coffee cup.

Kaylee approached Jessica at the counter. "Looks as if those two are hitting it off."

"Isn't it great?" Jessica beamed, then grew more serious.

"Any news from Phil yet?"

"No, not yet."

"Tad downloaded his mother's cell phone bill this morning. It lists calls right up to last Thursday night. I thought it'd be worth checking out the numbers in case the blackmailer contacted her by phone."

"Good idea. Where's the bill?"

"Tad has it."

Kaylee joined him at his table, where he was now studying his mother's cell phone bill. "See any numbers in there that might help us?" she asked.

"Yeah, maybe." He pointed to an entry on the bill. "She received a 45-second call less than half an hour before the robbery at the Newton place. She made a call as soon as that one ended, then sent a text to another number."

Kaylee recognized the last number. "That's her friend Sara's number. Sara said your mom texted her to change the time she'd planned to meet her date at the cafe." She scanned down to the next text, which was from Sara. "And this must've been when Sara texted her to make sure she was okay." Kaylee pointed to several texts and incomplete calls that had registered on Friday from a single number. "Are these from you?"

Tad nodded. "I guess the quickest way to figure out who those other numbers belong to is to call them." The young man appeared slightly sheepish when he asked, "Sorry, but can I use your phone? I still don't have one."

Kaylee hesitated. It might be the quickest way, but was it the safest?

"If the person at the other end picks up, I'll act as if I have the wrong number," Tad said.

Kaylee reluctantly acquiesced and handed him her phone. The first number he keyed in went unanswered. Same for the second number. Tad gave her phone back.

"I can ask my NSA friend to find out who the numbers belong to," Kaylee said. "It shouldn't be much trouble for his people."

Tad tensed. "You won't tell him about me being here, will you?"

"No." Kaylee glanced around the shop. "But you grew up here. Half these people must've recognized you. Your presence on the island is hardly a secret."

He shrugged. "I guess. I didn't count on a fed already being in Turtle Cove."

"He's looking for the truth. That's what you want to know, isn't it?"

Tad studied his coffee mug for a long moment. "Yes."

"May I?" She pointed to the printout of his mother's phone bill.

He handed it to her. "Sure. Go ahead."

She tucked it into her purse, then stood. "I need to open my shop next door, but I'll call Jess as soon as I learn anything."

As she stepped outside, she nearly collided with Reese on the sidewalk.

"Whoa." He put out a hand to steady her. "What are you up to?"

She told him about the call list. "I'm going to ask Phil to look up the numbers."

Reese fell into step beside her as she walked toward The Flower Patch.

When her phone rang, she was tempted to let it go to voice mail, but a glance at the screen changed her mind. "This is one of the numbers we just tried to call." She hit the answer button. "Hello?"

"Hey, did you try to call this number?"

"Yes, who is this?"

"My name's Abe. I work at Filibuster in Turtle Cove."

It was the restaurant Kaylee had trailed Phil to on Tuesday morning, and apparently the one the admiral and his son and aide had eaten at Thursday night.

Abe continued talking. "I was throwing out the trash and heard a ringing sound in the Dumpster, but I didn't get to the phone in time to answer it. It took me a couple minutes to find it and call you back. I figured maybe you lost this phone or know who it belongs to."

Kaylee didn't actually know who it belonged to, but she certainly could think of three prime suspects who'd dined there last week. "I'll be right over to pick it up. Thank you so much."

Reese, who'd been listening in on the call, fixed a stern gaze on her. "What if it's a setup?"

Kaylee shrugged. "That's a risk I think we have to take."

18

Reese lagged behind on the sidewalk to make a call while Kaylee let herself into The Flower Patch. She found Mary in the workroom arranging a birthday bouquet and gave her an update on Tabitha's phone bill and the call from Abe at Filibuster. As Kaylee was thanking Mary for agreeing to watch Bear for a little while, Reese entered the room.

"The restaurant's hostess confirmed they have an Abe working in the kitchen," he announced, holding his phone aloft. "He got in half an hour ago."

"Great," Kaylee said. "Unless the entire staff at the restaurant is crooked, I'm sure I'll be safe."

"I'd still like to go with you," Reese said.

Despite her bravado, butterflies had been fluttering around Kaylee's middle ever since she'd answered Abe's call, so she wasn't about to protest. "That would be nice."

"You should probably inform Phil," Reese added begrudgingly. "He may want to check out what else got thrown in that Dumpster and dust the phone for prints."

"Good thinking."

Kaylee made the call as Reese drove them to Filibuster. She also gave Phil the numbers from the phone bill for his people to check out, then hung up. Reese parked near the Dumpster, and Kaylee scanned the rooflines.

"I don't see any security cameras around here," she said. "Do you?"

Reese's gaze went to the eaves of the surrounding buildings. "Nope. It couldn't be that easy."

Abe met them at the kitchen's back door and pulled the phone from his apron pocket. He wore latex gloves.

"Were you wearing the gloves when you fished the phone out of the Dumpster?" Kaylee asked him.

"Yeah, why?"

"So your fingerprints won't be on the phone?" Reese clarified.

Abe shook his head. "No."

"Did anyone else handle the phone?" Kaylee asked.

Abe's eyes widened. "No. Only me. Was it stolen? Because if you were hoping to find a purse or anything else in the Dumpster, I'm afraid the garbage truck just came by and emptied it. You're lucky you called the phone when you did or I wouldn't have found it."

Phil arrived then and asked Abe a few more questions, but the young man had no other information of value.

After Phil finished examining the Dumpster, Kaylee asked him, "Were your people able to find out who the phone belongs to?"

"No, it's a burner phone. Pay-as-you-go." Phil pulled out his mobile phone, opened a text message, and read it. "Purchased in Seattle six weeks ago and activated four weeks ago."

"Someone called Tabitha from this phone minutes before the burglary," Kaylee reminded him. "So if you're convinced she's the one who broke into the Newtons' house, it seems likely the call was to tell her it was time."

Phil's head cocked curiously. "What makes you think someone told her to do the job?"

"What makes *me* think? You're the one who suggested she was a sleeper spy that had been activated."

Or was she blackmailed? Kaylee glanced at Reese, wondering if she was doing the right thing keeping Tad's arrival—as well as the note Tad claimed to have found—a secret from Phil.

"Then again," she said, her mind suddenly spinning with

other scenarios, "the admiral and his son and his aide were all at this restaurant at the time the call was made. So what if one of them gave her the all clear and then disposed of the phone in the Dumpster? Shawn seems convinced Ryan was somehow behind the break-in, right?"

Phil's eyes lit and after a moment of mental calculation, he nodded. "Six weeks ago fits when Ryan flew into Seattle and made his way here. I'd have to check the admiral's itinerary for that time period to see if he or his aide could've been there at that time too."

"Did you get an ID on the number Tabitha phoned after receiving the call from this burner phone?" Kaylee asked.

"No, and we couldn't trace where that phone was bought either."

"Is that unusual?" Kaylee asked.

Phil grimaced. "It could mean we're looking at organized crime."

Or foreign spies. Kaylee cringed.

"Or a federal agency?" Reese asked.

"Yeah, maybe she called the FBI agent who picked her up at the ferry," Kaylee said. "Couldn't the FBI ensure a phone is untraceable?"

Phil nodded once more, although he didn't appear as if he liked to admit government agencies would keep each other in the dark . . . or maybe that another agency could slip anything past the NSA's notice.

"What are you going to do now, Phil?" Kaylee asked.

"Nothing that concerns you."

Kaylee tamped down a surge of irritation. "Until I know Tabitha is safe, I'm going to be concerned. Face it: you wouldn't know as much as you do if not for us."

Reese's warm arm slipped securely around her shoulder.

Whether it was to calm her or show his solidarity, she wasn't sure, but her gratitude for his presence swelled.

Phil appeared borderline exasperated now as he glanced from her to Reese and back to her. "I appreciate your help," he finally said through gritted teeth.

"I'm glad to hear it." She felt increasingly emboldened with Reese holding his ground beside her. "Because I have an idea for how you can flush Ryan out."

"Do you think Ryan could've charmed Tabitha into breaking into his parents' house for him to give himself an alibi?" Phil asked.

Kaylee shrugged. "I don't know Tabitha. But I have an easier time believing some slimeball blackmailed her into doing it than that she is actually a spy."

"It stands to reason that one of the three men from Pennybrook Grove who had dinner here that night made the call," Reese interjected. "The only people who could've supplied Tabitha with the home's security code were the admiral, his wife, their son, and his aide."

Phil sighed. "Okay, what's your idea?"

Kaylee grinned. "We pay the family a visit and plant the phone in Ryan's pocket. Then while all three men are present, we dial the number and see how everyone reacts."

Phil was skeptical. "I doubt any of them would be foolish enough to give themselves away."

"Maybe not in so many words, but their microexpressions will," Kaylee argued. "Think about it. Whoever tossed that phone has to believe it's buried under a mountain of garbage by now. He's going to know someone planted it in his pocket and that he needs to do a better job of covering his trail."

"Assuming we put it in the right culprit's pocket," Phil said.

"If we don't," Kaylee added, "then the real culprit will try to stack the evidence against the wrong guy, don't you think?"

"Maybe," Phil agreed grudgingly.

"What do we have to lose?" Kaylee asked.

"If we're wrong, the admiral's confidence in me for starters." Phil huffed. "Not to mention the fact that we found the phone, which could tip off the real culprit into covering his tracks even better."

"You got any other ideas?" Reese asked.

Phil glanced at his wristwatch. "Not at the moment. I'll call you at four. Your camp is finished by then, right?"

"Yes," Kaylee said.

"Okay," Phil said. "If I haven't tracked down more leads by then, we'll go with your idea."

"Sounds good." Kaylee only just managed to keep her sense of victory from edging into her voice.

With a sharp nod, Phil strode to his truck, climbed in, and roared out of the parking lot.

"We're on the verge of a breakthrough," Kaylee said as she watched him leave. "I know it."

Reese reached over and squeezed her hand. "I hope so."

The second-to-last afternoon of the spring break camp zipped by, and all of the students were enthralled by their field trip to The Flower Patch. With Jessica and DeeDee to help, Kaylee and Mary led the children on a tour of the shop, then helped them create small arrangements to take home. Sara's mother's health had taken a turn for the worse, so the teacher had bowed out of the day's activities.

By quarter after four, all their campers had been collected by their parents, but Phil still hadn't phoned.

"Where's Tad?" Kaylee asked Jessica as they cleaned up the workroom.

A mile-wide smile stretched across Jessica's lips. "He and Mila went whale watching, hoping to catch sight of the new babies."

DeeDee raised an eyebrow. "I guess you're hoping his being here will rekindle the old flame?"

"A mother can hope," Jessica replied. "He is such a nice young man."

"But it doesn't sound as if he plans on seeking a type of job that would keep him in the Pacific Northwest," Mary said.

Jessica's smile dropped. "That is the one downside. But if it's meant to be, they'll make it work."

"Time will tell," Kaylee said.

Jessica glanced at the clock. "Speaking of time, you should phone Phil."

"Okay." Kaylee placed the call while the others gathered around to listen in.

Phil answered on the first ring. "I was about to call you. I figured I should give you an extra few minutes for your students to clear out."

"Then you've decided to go with my idea?" Kaylee held up crossed fingers.

A heavy sigh hissed across the line. "Yes." Phil explained how he envisioned it playing out. "Can you meet me at Tabitha's in twenty minutes?"

"On my way."

"I'll take Bear to my house." DeeDee reached for his leash. "You can pick him up when you're done. I've got a big pot of chili we can have for dinner while you tell us what happened."

Phil was waiting for Kaylee in Tabitha's driveway. "One of my staff has spoofed Tabitha's number so that when she gets my signal and calls the phone, it will look like Tabitha is calling."

Kaylee took a deep breath and climbed into his truck. "Okay, let's do this."

The men and Mrs. Newton were already seated in the living room when Phil and Kaylee came in. "I've told the family you have a theory about the break-in you'd like to present to them," Phil said to Kaylee, loud enough to announce their arrival.

Kaylee's heart kicked into double time. When she'd dreamed up the idea of planting the phone in Ryan's pocket, she hadn't considered she'd need an excuse to be there ahead of the phone ringing. She was grateful that Phil had . . . but he hadn't told her what to say. He probably figured she could wing it, since she always had one theory or another whipping through her mind.

Expelling a deep breath, she decided to play all her cards. "As you know, your neighbor Tabitha Mason has been missing since the night of your break-in."

Everyone nodded.

"What you don't know—what even Phil doesn't know . . ."

He froze, his thumb hovering over the screen of his cell phone.

Hoping he wasn't so thrown by her bombshell he forgot to signal his compatriot, Kaylee plunged on. "What you don't know is Tabitha left behind a note for her son. We found it in a secret hiding place in her house. It claims she was being blackmailed. She clearly feared for her life and—"

The buzz of the burner phone cut off what Kaylee had been about to say. The timing couldn't have been more perfect. But no one in the room reacted to the sound. When it buzzed a second and a third time, no one made a move to check their phones.

Kaylee looked at Ryan. "Did you want to answer that?"

"What?"

The phone buzzed again.

Kaylee pointed to the hoodie slung over the back of his chair, where the sound was clearly originating. "Your phone."

He couldn't have manufactured a more believable blank expression if he was a trained actor. "Not mine. I have a jazz ringtone."

"It's coming from your jacket pocket," Diane said sharply.

This time, Ryan's forehead furrowed as his attention turned to his hoodie. He dug out the phone and held it in an open palm, studying it. "This isn't mine. Is it one of yours?"

Everyone else shook their head, and to Kaylee's disappointment, not one of them appeared the least bit fidgety.

"Answer it," Phil ordered. "Find out what the caller wants."

Ryan did as he was told. A moment later, he muffled the phone against his chest. "It's Tabitha."

"Tabitha!" Kaylee reached for the phone. "Let me talk to her." By the time Kaylee pressed the phone to her ear, the phone had gone dead. "She hung up."

"Why would Tabitha be calling you?" Phil asked Ryan.

"I told you," Ryan insisted. "It's not my phone."

"It was in your pocket," Shawn argued. "Who else's could it be? It's got to be like I figured. Only you didn't bribe the woman—you blackmailed her to pull off the theft while we were all at dinner, giving you an airtight alibi."

Diane gasped.

Admiral Newton scowled at his son. "Is this true?"

"No!" Ryan sprang from his chair.

Phil moved to intercept him. "Where are you going?"

Ryan pointed to the sideboard, or more specifically to the phone on top of it. "To get *my* phone." Phil stepped aside and Ryan retrieved his phone. He tapped in the password, then presented the phone to his dad. "This is my phone. I don't know whose that is. Probably some fake Shawn slipped into my pocket to frame me."

Shawn catapulted to his feet. "How dare you make such an accusation!"

Ryan stared him down. "You think I did it. You said so in front of a room full of witnesses. Trouble is, you have no proof. Not much of a stretch to imagine you'd stage this little charade to stonewall me."

"That's enough!" the admiral roared. "Sit down, both of you." He turned his wrath on Phil. "I don't know whose phone this is or who that Mason woman purports to have blackmailed her. But the fact remains that other than myself, no one, not even my wife, knows my safe combination. Yet it was open when we returned to the house. Is this Tabitha person some sort of safecracker?"

Kaylee's thoughts flashed to the image of Tabitha on the dashcam footage DeeDee recovered. "Spy cameras are minuscule these days," she said to the admiral. "One could've been strategically located where it would record you opening your safe."

"But how?" Mrs. Newton interjected. "No one other than my husband, Ryan, and Shawn had been in the house."

With a glance at Ryan, Kaylee said, "I don't mean any disrespect, Mrs. Newton, but your son seems to date a lot of different women."

Mrs. Newton's face blanched while her husband's turned three shades of red.

"Ryan," Admiral Newton demanded, "did you have a woman in this house?"

He shrugged. "Sure, one or two, but we were never in your office." Ryan's eyes sprang wider and he pierced Shawn with a suspicious look. "But I wouldn't put it past Shawn giving her a tour."

"Her as in Tabitha Mason?" Phil clarified.

Ryan shook his head. "No, I told you before, I've never met the woman."

"Believe me, sir," Shawn said to the admiral, "I would never compromise your security by giving a visitor a tour of your office."

"But either one of you could've set up the camera to learn the safe's combination, then passed it on to your accomplice," Phil said.

Shawn and Ryan fired off arguments immediately, only to be silenced by the admiral bellowing, "Quiet!" When his command was followed, he added, "Let's see about this." Admiral Newton headed to his office and the rest of them followed.

Kaylee hovered at the doorway, Ryan and Shawn stood glowering on one side of the office, and the rest speculated about potential hiding spots for a camera. Looking at Ryan's and Shawn's faces, Kaylee was becoming less convinced they'd set up a camera. And if it had been a visitor, it would've had to have been something that would seem perfectly innocent left lying around. Something Tabitha could've easily recovered before leaving.

Kaylee mentally drew lines of sight from the safe to nearby shelves. "Are you right- or left-handed?" she asked the admiral.

"Left. Why?"

"You've been searching the wrong side of the room." Kaylee walked to the safe and spun the combination dial with her left hand, showing how the only vantage point would be from the right wall.

Phil scanned the shelf on the wall to the right of the safe. "There's a disturbed dust pattern. Something was here and someone removed it. Did any of you take anything from here?"

Everyone denied it.

The admiral sank into the chair behind his desk. "So you're suggesting that whoever set up the camera used it to get my combination and then gave it and the house's alarm code to this Tabitha woman?"

"That's our working theory, yes," Phil said. "He likely

instructed her to activate the alarm by breaking a window before she left so you would get a call from the security company while still at dinner, giving all three of you an alibi."

"It wasn't me," Ryan blurted.

"And why would we believe you?" Shawn asked. "You can't hold a job for more than six months. You gamble beyond your means. Then you dip into your dad's wallet to pay for a date—if you pay for it at all and don't just leave the lady with the bill."

After a searing glare at Shawn, Ryan turned to his father, his voice pleading. "I know you have no reason to believe me. Yes, I've helped myself to the odd twenty, but I'd never steal government secrets and sell them to the enemy. You know me. You raised me to be more patriotic than that." He motioned toward Shawn. "But how well do you know him? He's only been with you for, what, three months?"

The admiral nodded slowly, appearing more confounded by the minute.

"I think Shawn planted the phone in my coat," Ryan went on, "because he knew you'd have an easy time believing I could cheat you and sweet-talk a woman into doing just about anything. And he knew I was on to him."

"On to me?" Shawn exclaimed. "That's ridiculous. What do you have on me?"

"I saw you talking to my girlfriend, giving her the grand tour the last time I had her to the house, and then again when she was here with this one"—Ryan jerked his thumb in Kaylee's direction—"and all those kids."

Kaylee's mind clambered to catch up to what he was saying. She wildly cast a glance in Phil's direction. Who was Ryan talking about? It couldn't have been DeeDee, which meant he had to be talking about Sara. But they hadn't gone out until this week. Or had they? *Surely Sara would've told me if she'd been out with Ryan before. If she'd been to his house. Wouldn't she?*

"What girlfriend are we talking about here?" Phil demanded.

"Sara," Ryan said, as if it should be obvious. "I saw her that night too. After Dad and Shawn left the restaurant and I finished my dinner, I walked down to the ferry and I saw her meet the blonde in the picture."

"Tabitha?" Kaylee frowned, confused. "But you said you didn't know her when I showed her picture."

"I didn't *know* her. But I recognized her and I figured I ought to find out what Sara was doing talking to her before I said anything. Unlike *some* people," he added with a glare in Shawn's direction, "I didn't want to cast unsubstantiated aspersions."

"Big words for a bum who can't keep a job," Shawn muttered.

Ignoring the aide's grumbling, Phil said, "We know about Sara's meeting with Tabitha at the ferry."

Yes, Sara had told them that much, but Kaylee's gut churned at the thought of what she'd neglected to tell them. Had she merely been embarrassed to admit she'd been dating a womanizer like Ryan? Kaylee replayed Monday's visit to the estate in her mind. Both Shawn and Ryan had talked to Sara at different times.

The admiral zeroed in on Shawn. "What did this Sara woman say to you? Did she admire how important your job is?"

Shawn shrugged. "She might've."

"And did it not occur to you she could've been flirting with you for information, once she realized my son didn't have access to what she was after?"

Shawn's eyes widened. "But Sara didn't break in here. The blonde next door did." He looked to Phil. "Didn't she?"

"The dropped business card containing her prints is the only evidence it was her," Phil said. "But someone could've deliberately planted it to frame her."

Kaylee's relief that Tabitha was moving lower on Phil's

suspect list was tempered by the sickening realization that Sara was climbing higher on it.

"Did Sara ask you about your work for the admiral?" Phil asked Shawn.

The man's expression changed from shock to surprise. "Yeah, come to think of it, she did."

"She's a schoolteacher," Kaylee said in Sara's defense. "She's curious by nature."

With a sharp glance at Kaylee, Phil said, "I think we'd better be going."

He thanked the admiral and the others for their time, then grasped Kaylee's elbow and hurried her from the house.

"What's wrong with you?" Kaylee asked as they reached his truck, wrenching her arm out of his grip.

"I know you want to believe in Sara, but can I remind you of one thing first?"

"What?" Kaylee practically spat the word.

"Your *friend* Sara was planning the spring break camp activities with you, correct?"

"Yes."

"And yet you'd failed to track down the owner of Pennybrook Grove to gain permission to visit the island's oldest tree."

Kaylee's heart sank.

Phil crossed his arms. "Doesn't it strike you as suspicious that Sara didn't admit to knowing the owner's son?"

Kaylee swallowed hard. Sara hadn't arrived at their meeting yet the night Mila told them to ask Tabitha, but Sara must have known before then that DeeDee was struggling to contact the owner. And that wasn't even the worst of it.

As Tabitha's friend, Sara would know *exactly* how to blackmail her.

19

By the time Kaylee arrived at DeeDee's to let her know how the "sting" had gone, everyone else was there too, including Reese, Mary and Herb, Jessica and Luke, and Mila and Tad. But they must've been able to read Kaylee's wariness from her expression, because their excited energy fizzled to a subdued hush within moments of her walking through the door.

Reese took her coat and commiserated with, "I guess it didn't go as we'd hoped?"

Kaylee gratefully accepted the warm cup of tea DeeDee offered her and took a long sip before responding. "You're not going to believe who our number one suspect is now." She shook her head. "*I* still can't believe it." They all took a seat around the extended kitchen table and Bear crept up into Kaylee's lap, as if he knew she needed extra moral support. Then one by one, Kaylee laid out the allegations and evidence that all pointed to Sara.

When she finished, Andy let out a long whistle that seemed to express everyone's shock.

"There's got to be some other explanation," Mary said. "The woman faithfully came and helped out at camp during her vacation, with the exception of today. That doesn't sound like the actions of someone selling top secret documents to a foreign government."

"I've got to agree," Jessica said. "Ryan is a slick one. I wouldn't put it past him to pick Sara out of a crowd, like a lion prowling for the weakest animal in the herd—the one he can take down with the least effort. He was probably setting her up as the fall guy for his theft from the start."

"That's definitely a possibility," DeeDee added. "I don't think Sara has dated much, so it probably wasn't difficult for someone as smooth as Ryan to manipulate her with his charm."

Tad appeared skeptical. "You think so? I'm not saying I think Sara would blackmail my mom, but the few times I met her, she always struck me as really smart. Not the kind of person who'd let herself be duped by a guy trying to impress her."

Mila shifted in her seat. "It is weird, though, that she didn't mention her relationship with Ryan when she knew you guys were trying to get permission to take a field trip to the estate."

"Maybe she didn't realize that's where the oldest tree was," Herb offered.

"I think I know one way to test how truthful she's been with us." Kaylee drew Tabitha's phone bill from her purse and smoothed it open. "Sara claimed Tabitha texted her sometime after seven last Thursday night to say all was well." Kaylee scanned the column of sent messages and shook her head. "But the last text Tabitha sent is listed as before the time of the break-in."

"Sounds as if Sara didn't think through how easy it would be to verify what she claimed," Reese said.

"Unless," Kaylee murmured, "Tabitha texted Sara from a different phone. Maybe the man who picked her up at the ferry let her borrow his."

DeeDee flipped back through her calendar. "There are a couple of other things that don't look good for Sara, though. She would've been in Seattle six weeks ago, when Phil says the burner phone was purchased there, because her mom had to have another surgery." DeeDee turned the calendar she'd been looking at so Kaylee could see. "I know, because Polly told me the school had to bring in another substitute teacher for her because her mom was in the hospital again. Since I was going to Seattle for a book convention that week, I stopped by the hospital and took Sara to lunch."

Kaylee pictured Sara going into the Newton house with Shawn Monday afternoon, allegedly so her young charge could use the restroom, and wondered if there'd been more to that little detour too.

"Kaylee?" Reese said, as if it weren't the first time.

Kaylee shook the thoughts from her mind. "I'm sorry. Did you ask something?"

"Yeah, I was wondering if Phil said what he was going to do next."

"No. I don't know if what we learned from Shawn and Ryan would be enough for him to secure a warrant for Sara's home to search for whatever was stolen. Maybe, given the risk to national security."

"Or they may opt to monitor her phone and e-mail account to try to catch her and her buyers red-handed," Luke suggested.

Jessica shivered. "I'm glad tomorrow's our last day of camp. It's going to be hard to act normal around her after all this."

"You have to," Reese said sternly. "You don't want to tip her off that anyone is onto her, or she may go underground and they'll never recover what was taken."

Kaylee gasped. "What if she already has? Maybe the story about her mother going into the hospital again and her not being able to make camp today was just that—a story."

Mary pulled out her phone. "That's easy enough to verify." She dialed what Kaylee presumed was the hospital and asked to be connected to Roxanne Wright's room. Mary ended the call with a "thank you," then said, "Roxanne Wright was released twenty minutes ago."

Kaylee ducked her head, feeling horrible for suggesting it could've merely been an excuse.

"You know," Tad said, "all her mother's health challenges have left Sara strapped for cash. I heard her talking to my mom about it when I was home at Christmas. It's not like teachers make a lot of money. Gives her a strong motive."

"But do you really think she'd blackmail your mother? It sounds as if they were pretty close." Kaylee squinted at him, wondering once again if the blackmail scheme had been a hoax he made up along with the letter he'd claimed to have found left behind by his mother.

"If she was desperate enough, yeah," he said instead. "I just hope my mom *is* in hiding like her note says."

Kaylee sighed. So did she.

Kaylee didn't hear from Phil the next morning and wondered whether he might have already taken Sara into custody. What would her mother do then?

But Sara showed up at the lighthouse keeper's quarters as usual for the afternoon's camp session.

"How's your mom feeling today?" Kaylee asked.

"Much better. Thanks for asking." Sara immersed herself in activities with the children, making it easy for the rest of the Petal Pushers to not betray their suspicions of her.

But by cleanup time, Kaylee could no longer contain her curiosity. She approached Sara, who was collecting some craft supplies, and asked, "Sara, can I ask you about that last text Tabitha sent you, about her having a great time? Did the text come from her phone?"

Sara's gaze shifted up, left then right, as if searching her memory bank and then perhaps composing a plausible explanation. "No, now that you mention it. I think the text started with 'This is Tabitha,' so it must've come from a different number."

Sara pulled out her phone and scrolled through her text history. "I must've assumed it was her date's phone. I can't believe I didn't realize the significance of that sooner. We should be able to trace the number." Sara frowned at her phone and scrolled the opposite direction through her message list. "Ugh, it's gone. I must've erased it."

Kaylee debated whether to accept Sara's claim at face value. After all, Tabitha might've been concerned that Sara would wonder why she never showed at the café. Or if she hadn't willingly gotten into the car with the FBI agent, she might've told her captor Sara would be worried. Then again, either way, if the text wasn't a complete fabrication on Sara's part, it certainly hadn't been a reply to Sara's text as she'd implied when she first mentioned it.

Before Sara's phone screen went blank, Kaylee speed-read the last text Sara had received. The number had no contact name assigned to it. The message said: *Haida Point, 5 o'clock.*

Kaylee's heart thumped. Was she meeting a buyer? Ryan? Shawn?

Sara pocketed her phone. "What made you think to ask about that text now, after all this time?"

"Oh." Kaylee fluttered her hand as if it was of no major consequence, but couldn't help noticing the way it trembled. Hopefully Sara had missed it. "Um, we managed to download Tabitha's cell phone records in hopes it would help us locate her," Kaylee fudged, since they hadn't told Sara that Tad was in town. "And there were no records of any calls or messages after the one she sent you before her date."

"Ah, I see." Sara's tone sounded hurt that Kaylee had doubted her story.

"I figured she must've used her date's phone," Kaylee quickly said.

Sara lifted the now full bin of craft supplies. "Well, I think that's it for me. This camp was fun. See you ladies later."

The instant the door closed behind Sara, Kaylee whipped out her phone.

"Who are you calling?" Jessica asked.

Kaylee told them about the text she'd seen on Sara's phone, then repeated the explanation to Phil over the phone. "It could be a meet to sell the stolen goods."

"Thanks for the heads up," Phil said. "I trust I don't need to remind you to stay away? If we hope to catch both Sara and her contact, we can't afford for either party to get spooked."

Haida Point was a wooded, rocky bluff off Deer Harbor Road—private, but not the kind of place that would be conducive to a quick getaway.

"I wouldn't dream of interfering," Kaylee promised.

"Hey," DeeDee said, as Kaylee disconnected her call. "Sara's text may have said Haida Point, but she's signaling to go the opposite direction." DeeDee pointed out the window toward the end of the lighthouse's long driveway, where Sara was waiting to turn onto the road.

Kaylee grabbed her coat and Bear's leash. "Do you mind locking up here? I think I should follow her."

"Of course not, go," Jessica urged.

Kaylee and Bear jumped in her car and swerved onto the road in time to see Sara's car veer off a little farther up. As quickly as traffic would allow, Kaylee closed the distance to where Sara had turned, but there was no sign of Sara's hatchback. Kaylee headed down the street, scanning parking lots and driveways, and pausing at each new intersection to peer in both directions. Three intersections later, Bear let out an excited yip.

"What do you see?" Kaylee leaned across the seat to track the direction of his gaze. Through the shrubbery, she could make out a redhead—*Sara!*—climbing out of her car. "Good catch, boy."

Kaylee pulled to the side of the street and scanned the large property, which was flanked by scraggly bushes and a dilapidated chain-link fence. "Looks like a scrapyard. Bear, you stay here while I go check it out, okay?" She locked the car door and pushed it closed as quietly as she could to avoid attracting Sara's attention.

Kaylee walked along the fence, peering through the shrubs, until she spotted Sara again. She was heading deeper into the yard with long, brisk strides, as if she knew exactly where she was headed.

When Sara went left in front of a row of old station wagons, Kaylee hopped the fence and slipped along a parallel row so she could continue to see without being seen.

Sara opened the rear door of a green-and-brown, panel-style wagon and shoved her hand under the seat.

Is this where her accomplice stashed the admiral's burgled goods? Kaylee snapped a photograph with her phone.

A moment later, Sara backed out of the car holding a foil-wrapped package the size of a digital tablet. Kaylee took three more pictures before Sara concealed the package beneath her coat.

Kaylee's phone chose that moment to buzz in her hand. Ducking behind a rusty pickup, she scrambled to mute the phone, thankful she'd at least had it in vibrate mode for camp.

"Who's there?" Sara demanded.

For the briefest moment, Kaylee debated confronting Sara about what was in the package she'd retrieved. But if the woman was crooked enough to blackmail Tabitha, then there was no telling how she'd react. Better to let her decide she hadn't heard anything after all.

Sara's footfalls soon headed back in the direction she'd come from, but Kaylee didn't want to risk poking her head up to track her progress. Instead, she took a moment to send the incriminating pictures she'd snapped to Phil with their location. *I suspect she's heading your way,* Kaylee added. The message sent, she carefully peered around over the truck's hood.

Her breath caught in her throat.

Sara stood in the next aisle, scanning vehicles.

Kaylee ducked back into the shadows at the same moment her phone lit up, indicating an incoming call from Phil. She accepted the call but pocketed the phone, hoping he would hear something useful. In the distance, Bear was yipping impatiently.

"I know you're there. Show yourself!" Sara demanded.

Holding her breath, Kaylee shrank into the narrow space between the pickup shielding her from Sara's view and the one beside it.

A dark shadow fell over her. Sara stood there with a heavy metal rod in her hand. The schoolteacher let out a disgusted snort. "I should've known it would be you."

Kaylee attempted to stand, but she'd wedged herself too tightly in the confined space. "Why are you doing this?"

"What is it you think I'm doing?" Sara practically spat the question.

Kaylee quickly decided telling her everything she knew would be the best way to convince the woman her plan was already foiled, and she might as well surrender now. Kaylee wriggled forward, and this time managed to regain her feet. "I assume that you're collecting what you blackmailed Tabitha into stealing for you." Kaylee straightened to her full height, as if unconcerned by the fact Sara still had her cornered between the cars.

Sara cackled, although there was enough of a crack in the sound to convince Kaylee she'd gotten to the woman. "Tabitha was a perfect angel. What could I possibly have on her to blackmail her with?"

"The fact that her brother had been a Russian spy. It'd be enough to make the feds think twice about trusting Tad."

Sara's eyebrows lifted. "My, my, you have been busy. Who

would've thought the cheap cell phone I bought for my mom during her last stay in Seattle would've come in so handy? I disguised my voice and Tabitha had no clue it was me."

"So you had nothing to do with her disappearance?" Kaylee was pretty sure Tabitha had contacted the FBI, unbeknownst to Sara—and apparently to the admiral and NSA as well—but if Sara hadn't kidnapped Tabitha, wouldn't she be worried about where Tabitha was? If not as a concerned friend, then certainly as someone who wanted to know where the woman she'd blackmailed into stealing important government secrets had gone.

"Nope," Sara said. "But it worked out well for me, don't you think? I figured she was so afraid she'd be caught for breaking into the Newtons' place she went into hiding. And disappearing like that made her look even guiltier."

"Until DeeDee secured the dashcam footage showing Tabitha being picked up by a couple of men. You alone knew they weren't her blackmailers or buyers, so you had to assume she'd been in contact with someone who'd be watching the package."

"Sure. But by the time Tabitha told them the kid on the bike had lifted it, he'd already passed it on to my mom."

The bag lady. "And she hid the package here?" While Kaylee kept Sara talking, she inched out of the corner, hoping Sara wouldn't notice.

"Yup." Sara grinned. "The hiding place was Mom's idea, in fact. Being sick so long, she's had lots of time to pick up tips from all the crime shows."

"But you're the one who chucked the cell phone in the Dumpster?"

Sara's face blanched and her grip on the pipe tightened. "How'd you know about that?"

"The number may not have been traceable to you, but it still appeared in Tabitha's call history. So I called it, and an employee at the restaurant heard it ringing in the trash."

Sara's face instantly went from white to red. "There's nothing to connect that phone to me!"

"Except that you were in Seattle when it was purchased six weeks ago. Did you remember to wear gloves when you inserted the SIM card? Or will the feds find your fingerprints inside the phone?"

"You're bluffing. If the feds had anything on me, they would've arrested me already."

"What makes you think they aren't waiting at Haida Point to do just that? How do you know your buyer isn't a federal agent?"

"Shut up!" Sara smashed her steel pipe against the truck's hood, denting the metal.

Kaylee decided to press her luck. "Your fatal mistake was not telling us you knew Ryan when we were trying to make contact with the owners of Pennybrook Grove."

"I said, *shut up!*" Sara smashed the windshield next to Kaylee's head.

Kaylee shielded her face with her arm. "I'm trying to help you." She pointed to the bulge in Sara's jacket. "If you turn yourself in now, before that gets into the wrong hands, I'm sure the judge will be more lenient on you."

"Yeah? And will he pay my mother's medical bills too?"

"That's why you're doing this? To pay hospital bills?"

"You hadn't figured that part out, Miss Marple? You must be slipping. Motive, means, and opportunity. Isn't that what you're supposed to look for when you solve a crime? I would've thought my motive would be obvious."

Kaylee sighed. "Yes, but there are other ways of—"

"No!" Sara raised the steel rod threateningly. "This is the only way."

20

The steel rod smashed against Kaylee's raised arm and she screamed in pain.

The next instant, Reese charged over the side of the truck and hurled himself at Sara. They landed in a heap in the dirt. He wrestled the bar from Sara's hands, then rolled her onto her front and yanked her arms behind her back. "Pull the shoelaces from her shoes," Reese said.

Kaylee fumbled with Sara's laces, then finally retrieved them and handed one string to Reese. While he secured Sara's hands, Kaylee tied her ankles. "How did you find me?"

"I was heading to the lighthouse to learn the latest when I saw you come this way, so I followed you. But I lost you on a turn and had to search the streets until I spotted your car again." Reese hauled Sara to a sitting position. "That's when I heard Sara yell, 'Who's there?'" Reese turned to Kaylee and folded her hands in his. "I hopped the fence, desperate to get to you before she did." Concern creased his forehead. He loosened his hold of one hand and stroked the hair from her face. "Are you hurt?"

Kaylee's heart thumped at the tenderness in his voice, which made her forget the painful bruise likely forming on her arm where Sara had hit her with the steel rod. "I'm fine." She leaned into his touch. "Thank you for being here. I don't know what I—"

Reese silenced her with a fingertip to her lips. "You're okay now. That's all that matters." His eyes searched hers and a flock of butterflies let loose in her belly.

She cupped her hand over his and he held it against his chest, where she could feel his heart pounding just like hers.

He drew her closer, his head dipping.

Her heart soared as she tipped her face up to receive Reese's kiss . . . but their lips never met.

"Aren't you worried your bad guy might get away while you're busy fraternizing?" Phil's voice boomed from twenty yards away, interrupting the moment.

Kaylee and Reese sprang apart and simultaneously looked at Sara, who'd somehow managed to loop her arms to her front and was busily unbinding her ankles with her still-tied hands. An instant later, she had them loose and surged to her feet.

Reese caught her by the arm. "Where do you think you're going?"

Phil took charge of Sara and secured her with handcuffs. "It was smart thinking calling me, Kaylee," he said. "I recorded Sara's entire confession as I raced here."

Kaylee removed her phone from her pocket and disconnected the call at last. "Whatever she made Tabitha steal is inside her jacket."

Phil pulled on latex gloves and retrieved the package. He opened the foil pouch and removed a small black tablet.

"That's what all the navy's secrets are stored on?" Kaylee asked.

Phil chuckled. "Not exactly. After cutting through a nightmare of red tape, I managed to reach the FBI agent we saw with Tabitha in the surveillance footage. It turns out she called them in on this from the first blackmail call." Phil held up the tablet. "This is the dummy one the feds had her substitute for the real thing."

"So there was never any danger of naval secrets being sold?" Reese clarified.

Phil nodded sharply. "Correct. Not that they bothered to inform the admiral or NSA. Their plan had been to catch the blackmailer at the handoff or at least mark him so they could eventually arrest him—I mean her—*and* the buyer."

"But they hadn't counted on the handoff going down the way it did," Kaylee guessed.

"Right. That's why they beat us to the surveillance tapes in the neighborhood. Not that it helped them. Of course, they'd put a tracking device in the tablet, so they thought they were still okay. But they hadn't counted on it being slipped into this makeshift Faraday cage to block any signals." He held up the foil and met Sara's gaze. "That was smart thinking."

She rolled her eyes, no doubt thinking she hadn't been smart enough.

"Anyway, when the package went dark, they decided to keep us in the dark too. They've been watching all communication traffic to and from the island for any hint of an exchange. They saw the anonymous sale ad online, and when days went by with no takers, they decided to pose as the buyers themselves and take her down."

Suddenly, vehicles swarmed the scrapyard. They swerved to block the exits, kicking up swirls of dust. Men and women in FBI jackets burst from the cars and aimed their weapons toward the little group, using their car doors as shields.

"Stand down." Phil held up his badge. "We've got your blackmailer in custody."

A man Kaylee recognized from the dashcam footage strode over and spoke with Phil in hushed tones, then relieved him of Sara. Another agent collected the tablet from Phil and handed him another shielded package, presumably holding the real thing. "Thanks for your help," the agent said.

Within minutes, the lot of them cleared out with Sara in tow, leaving just Phil, Reese, and Kaylee.

Stunned silent, Kaylee stared after them. Questions churning in her mind, and the most important one burst from her lips in a rush. "What about Tabitha? Where is she?"

Phil clapped her on the back. "I'm sure by the time you get back to town, she'll be reunited with her son."

Kaylee's attention snapped to Phil. "You knew he was here?"

He chuckled. "I'm NSA. The FBI may be able to keep us guessing for a while, but an intern can't."

Kaylee ducked her head. "I'm sorry I didn't tell you, but I was worried one of your own people might have kidnapped her. And as it turned out, reality wasn't that far off."

Phil smirked at her. "You're not that great a liar."

A laugh burst from Reese. He smothered it with, "I'm sorry, but it's true."

"Gee, thanks," Kaylee said.

Phil's smirk faded as he focused his gaze on Kaylee. "And speaking of your lack of poker face, your expression was very clear yesterday. Just forget what I said after that branch fell." He glanced at Reese. "I can tell I'm out of my league here."

"Take care, Phil," Kaylee said, then her ears picked up the sound of Bear's distant yipping. She hurried to her car and gave him a thorough cuddle, assuring him all was well.

Reese joined them. "Did you get the text from Jessica?"

"I've been a little too busy to check my phone." Kaylee grabbed it from her pocket. "She must be going crazy waiting for news."

"Actually, Tabitha's at the Roberts' house. Jessica invited us all over to celebrate. I'm sure they'll be eager to hear how we captured Sara too." Reese smiled broadly, sending Kaylee's tummy twirling.

She grinned. "I'll let you tell the story."

Half an hour later, The Petal Pushers and their friends and family gathered over a delicious taco dinner at Jessica and Luke's. Reese recapped his and Kaylee's experience at the scrapyard, and then Tabitha filled Kaylee and all her friends in on the days leading up to her undercover escapade.

"The plan had been to insert a female agent to pose as me for the burglary, but the agent hadn't yet arrived on the island when Sara told me it was time." Tabitha shook her head. "I still can't believe she used me like that."

"Why didn't you cancel your date after her call?" Tad asked his mom.

"Protective custody wasn't the original plan. I thought the FBI would catch the bad guys at the drop and then I could be on my way."

"You must've been terrified when Mrs. Newton walked in on you," DeeDee said.

"Oh yes. But it was a good thing she'd inadvertently reset the alarm I'd disarmed because I was supposed to trigger it on my way out." Tabitha squeezed her hands together. "My heart all but jumped out of my chest when the thing went off. I slammed the rock through the window anyway on reflex, even though she'd know it wasn't how I got in, which was supposed to be how it looked." She inhaled deeply. "Then I almost forgot to switch out the tablet for the one the FBI gave me. I had to hide the real thing in the false bottom of a flowerpot they'd left by my back door so no one would find it on me or in my house."

Kaylee remembered the flowerpot by the back door and the dry spot next to it, which must've been from the feds shifting it to retrieve the real tablet.

"After that, it was all I could do to drive sedately toward town with a police cruiser wailing toward my house," Tabitha finished.

"Did you leave the business card behind on purpose?" Jessica asked.

Tabitha laughed. "No. I'd been goofing around on the computer, toying with design ideas, using dummy names and numbers. I'd stuffed the sample card of my favorite design in my pocket so I could ask Ned what he thought of it."

"How'd you two meet?" Mila asked.

"He'd been designing a guesthouse for one of my housekeeping clients, and we started corresponding online. We really hit it off, so we decided to finally go on a real date."

Jessica gave her a big hug. "I'm so happy for you."

Tabitha's expression became forlorn. "I doubt he'll want to see me again after the way I stood him up."

"I wouldn't be so sure about that," Kaylee said. "He seemed really concerned when he found out you were missing."

"Do you really think so?" Tabitha's face shifted from pensive to hopeful. "Should I try asking him out again?"

Kaylee exchanged a glance with Mary, then said, "Some leaps of faith are worth taking."

Reese insisted on ensuring that Kaylee and Bear got home safely from Jessica's, so he followed her to Wildflower Cottage in his pickup and even walked her to her front door.

"I think I'll be safe from here," Kaylee said as she let Bear into the house. "With any luck, I'll at least last the night without getting caught up in another national security scandal."

"Here's hoping." Reese chuckled, then grew quiet, fixing his gaze on her face. "Kaylee, I . . ."

"Yes?" she said, suddenly feeling lightheaded at his expression, which was at once fierce and tender.

"I need to tell you something." Reese took a deep breath.

"Seeing you with Phil this past week scared me. It made me realize how much I've grown to care about you—deeply care about you." He brushed a lock of hair away from her eyes. "And it made me realize I don't want to lose you."

Kaylee's lips trembled into a smile. "You'll never lose my friendship, Reese."

His eyes searched hers. "But what if it could be more than friendship?"

Kaylee's breath caught in her throat. "I'd like that," she finally managed to whisper. "Very much."

Reese cradled her face in his palms and, as their lips touched, Kaylee's heart soared.

Bear suddenly appeared in a side window, yipping his approval.

Her forehead pressed to Reese's, Kaylee laughed. "Apparently he'd like that too," she murmured, then lifted her lips to meet Reese's again.